A Pause
in the Desert

Books by Oliver La Farge

Tribes and Temples (with Frans Blom)

Laughing Boy (Pulitzer Prize for best novel of the year)

Sparks Fly Upward

The Year-Bearer's People

Long Pennant

All the Young Men

The Enemy Gods

As Long as the Grass Shall Grow

The Copper Pot

War Below Zero (with Bernt Balchen and Corey Ford)

Raw Material

Santa Eulalia

The Eagle in the Egg

The Changing Indian (editor)

Cochise of Arizona

The Mother Ditch

Behind the Mountains

A Pictorial History of the American Indian

A Pause in the Desert

A Pause
in the Desert

A COLLECTION OF SHORT STORIES

BY

OLIVER LA FARGE

HOUGHTON MIFFLIN COMPANY BOSTON
THE RIVERSIDE PRESS CAMBRIDGE
1957

With the exception of "A Pause in the Desert," here published
for the first time, the stories in this book originally appeared in
various magazines. *The New Yorker:* "The Touch of Greatness,"
"By the Boys Themselves," "Mr. Skidmore's Gift," "La Spécialité
de M. Duclos," "Prelude to Reunion," "The Resting Place,"
"The Happy Indian Laughter," "The Brush of the Wings."
The Atlantic Monthly: "Old Century's River." *Cosmopolitan:*
"The Bystander." *The Forum:* "Spud and Cochise." *'48:* "The
Bright Faces." *Esquire:* "Thick on the Bay." *The Magazine of
Fantasy and Science Fiction:* "John the Revelator." *The Saturday
Evening Post:* "To Walk in the City Streets."

The Riverside Press

CAMBRIDGE • MASSACHUSETTS
PRINTED IN THE U.S.A.

Contents

A Pause
in the Desert

Old Century's River

ALMOST AS SOON AS HE FOUND THOSE TWO miraculous bottles of whiskey he knew that they meant the end, and were to be the means of it. He did not state this explicitly to himself, but felt it below the level of worded thoughts or of admission, as a wild animal knows that its end is coming, as an old jungle hand, by the time he had reached his age, should have learned to know.

He saw the little suitcase that contained them by pure accident, because one of his awkward, improvised crutches slipped as he was turning away, after he had cut his fourth heart of palm. Four hearts of palm weren't much of a supply, but that was all he had strength for now. It was better to go short, and be sure of making it back to his shelter and his mosquito net before dark. He turned slowly, one crutch slipped, he caught himself, and it was then that he saw the edge of the valise, under a low-growing ramón palm. His faded blue eyes studied it for several seconds while he remembered that Tolling had looked for it, and had said that, among other things, he had two bottles of good whiskey in it.

He lowered himself to the ground slowly, with elaborate care not to jar his bad leg. The slightest jolt, twist, or even just wrong position meant a white swirl of pain which was not quick in going away. Presently he was on the ground, his legs out in front of him, and had pulled the little suitcase into the open.

He felt the case gently with the palm of his hand, studying it. It was about eighteen inches long and a foot wide. It had been badly scratched, probably bounced off a couple of trees when it was thrown from the plane, and one end was slightly charred. Three weeks lying on the damp ground had done it no good. Still, you could recognize its quality, the quality of the leather, very unlike the soft surface of native Mexican tanning. The brass locks were neat and solid. The initials under the handle were clear, "J.H.T." Tolling's case all right, and because he had not yet given up his fight, he could think that it was too bad that by now Tolling and McDaniels, two young and healthy men, might well be dead, and to consider with a bit of triumph and a bit of laughter that he, old, injured, his system charged with God only knew how many tropical infections, was still alive and still fighting.

An Indian would have given up by now. An Indian's reason would have told him that it was all over days ago, and very reasonably he would have given up and avoided a lot of discomfort by deliberately dying, the way Indians know how to do. A white man goes beyond reason, not with hope so much as with determination, and so a lot of times he wins out when he ought not to. Thus the first thing he got out of finding the valise was a lift, not at that moment applying to his situation the meaning of the thing he had just admitted to himself, his belief that Tolling and Mc-

Daniels had failed to make it. He thought of their probable demise only as a contrast to his own survival, with the triumph that the aged, the sick, the disreputable feel over the downfall of the young, the strong, the correct.

He remembered the ridiculousness of being hired by those two young fellows to guide them in the air. He remembered their tale of gold cached in an ancient mound, and the map and the old letter they had to prove it. He knew better, but they offered him nice work, good pay, and a cut in everything they found, to fly around and identify places from the air, later to run their camp and supply train. In honesty he'd warned them that they were starting too late, with the rains coming on; but they wanted to make a scout now, and come back the next season. That was all right with him. Anyway, he'd long wanted to know what it was like to fly.

He sure as hell found out. Sick and frightened, right from the start. And then good and lost — everything looked so different from the air. All he could do was feel awful and hang on to himself, and hang on to the gleam of the river, when he could find it.

After the crash, Tolling had delayed awhile, looking for the valise, before he and McDaniels started out. He had hoped to find it, not only for the liquor, but because it contained personal papers and a large-scale map of Chiapas. Tolling set a lot of store by maps. The trouble was, he had looked too close to the wreckage of the plane. From where he sat, the old man could not see the clearing in which they had come down, but he could see, like shafts between the great trees, the glow of light which marked it. The clearing was of no interest to him. There was nothing edible growing there. Except where the plane had cut a swathe and made a scorched area, it was all oleander, high as a man.

They were dead and he was on his own, all right. He was

sorry about them. It had been fine, the way they dragged him away from the burning wreckage, the way they splinted him and fixed up his shelter under his directions, and the generosity with which they divided the salvaged supplies with him. They had wanted to try carrying him out, but he knew that that would never have worked. Even then, when they stood before him, ready to go, he'd figured that forty miles of this kind of bush, with the swamp to cross, was going to be tough going for a couple of complete greenhorns. The bearing of their failure upon his own situation began to impress him. To free his mind of it, he concentrated on the suitcase. He was a trifle lightheaded, not with the familiar fever of malaria, but with a giddiness and feeling of infection that came from the poisons being manufactured in his leg.

He tried the catches. The two locks snapped open. Good. He lifted the lid. The top layer of socks and some brightly striped drawers kept the rest of the contents snug. Under them were various papers in several bundles, the folded map, and the two bottles. He did not touch them, but sat studying the labels and seals. The best, bottled in bond, aged, one hundred proof, the kind of liquor the very existence of which a man completely forgot in the little towns of the back country, drinking barbed wire, *aguardiente*, most of the time, and Habanero when he was flush.

The pale golden-brown contents of the two bottles promised him pleasure and relief from pain. The continuous throbbing of his leg this last week had at first broken his sleep, and the last few nights had allowed him to doze only in snatches. With one of these under his belt . . .

Seldom in his life had he tasted liquor of this class, mostly that time he found gold and sold out, and went clear to Mexico City. It had been his plan to go to the States, with all the cash he had, but Mexico City had everything, even blondes. He suspected that that blonde of his was synthetic, but if so she had done a job of it. She was blonde all over. He frowned over her name. Rita — Rita something, claimed to be half Polish. She was expensive as hell, but worth every peso of it. The memory of those six weeks had stayed good for years. She'd gone in for all sorts of mixed drinks, but he had mistrusted them; that was when he got onto the fine Bourbon. It goes down like tea, and it's as strong as anything that ever hit your stomach.

He closed the valise. Drawing his machete, he cut a length of narrow, flexible liana. The act took two flips of the wrist. He handled his machete with old skill, but he paused between the strokes and afterwards set the blade down as though it were heavily weighted. There was no more strength in him. With the liana he slung the valise from his shoulder. Then he sheathed the machete and went through the long, careful, effortful process of getting to his feet and onto the crutches Tolling and McDaniels had made for him.

It was about a hundred feet from where he stood to his shelter. He had come so far only because he had cleaned out everything edible nearer, at least everything that grew in places open enough for him to penetrate. Cutting a path into the really thick places was quite beyond him in his condition. As he inched his way back, he made a remarkable picture. He wore a fairly new straw sombrero, set aslant on his longish white hair. His three weeks' beard was scraggly, curly, and nearly as white as the finer hair of his head. His face was deeply tanned, of a sickly color under the tan, lined and sunken.

He wore a strong khaki shirt and slacks, purchased with

the advance money the young men had given him, but these now looked as if he had had them for years. They were filthy. The shirt had several rips in it. The left trouser leg, over his bad leg, had been cut away at the knee. On his left foot, the newly purchased, high laced boot had likewise been cut away above the ankle, leaving a sort of shoe. In between was the splint, fashioned out of pieces of the wrecked plane and wrapped with materials which had become gray-black, fuzzy, rotting rags. In his left breast pocket, four slender, white hearts of palm stuck up like candy sticks. His machete and knife hung at his waist, the little valise, woefully heavy, slid around against his back and his side.

He concentrated on his panting progress, leaving for later the endless, rambling self-communions of a man who has been long alone.

The forest in front of him lightened, there were the same brilliant shafts and streaks ahead of him as had marked the neighborhood of the clearing. He came out on the edge of the river beside his shelter. He rested, looking at the river. It was familiar; a great part of his life had been spent along it. Its presence supported him.

Within easy distance of him were a number of traps, the simple arrangements of sticks the Indians make for catching the smallest animals. He scanned them carefully, without expectation; he'd been living and moving around here too long for the little creatures to be coming by.

His shelter was a simple affair of palm branches and a tarpaulin, a lean-to facing the river. One end was over the roots of a massive mahogany, the other was partly closed by a smaller tree. In a rise of ground between two roots was his bed, a pile of palm branches and a blanket with the mosquito net suspended above. Behind that, on the raised shelf of another root, were his rifle and his supplies. In front of the shelter was a meager pile of firewood beside the black circle of his fire. The edge of the circle was cut by a frying pan with a spoon in it and a blackened tin can, its top bent backwards to form a sort of handle.

His supplies were cached in the empty tin cans beside the rifle. In one was a small bag of salt and another bag containing a handful of rice. A second was half full of carefully saved cigarette stubs, and on top of them an empty quinine bottle containing two whole cigarettes. In others were some money, some pieces of newspaper, a dozen matches wrapped elaborately in part of an oilskin tobacco pouch, and a bottle of insect repellent, nearly empty. Between the bed and the fireplace stood a badly dented Army issue canteen, its upper part fire-blackened, lacking its canvas cover and its cup. Most of the cans showed the effects of fire. The rifle had a charred place on the stock. Along the barrel were a number of spots of rubbed-down rust.

After a moment's hesitation, he took out one of the whole cigarettes and laid it carefully on a root. He hefted the canteen, and was relieved to find it full. It had become difficult to remember whether he had stuck to his routine of working his way to the water and filling it before he went looking for food. He tended to his fire, uncovering the coals, laying on twigs and bark, fanning gently with his hat, until he had a dependable little flame.

Daylight would last at least an hour more, but already the river was beginning to fill with shadow, while the sunlight became sharper, more emphatic, on the far bank. The occasional bole of a great tree, exposed directly to the light, turned gold. The water was a living, dull metal, moving in an oily, quiet, powerful, yet sluggish way, with blue here and there in its swirls. The Chacaljá — the river had a dozen names, Spanish, Nahua, Mayan; from among them this one, the one the Indians of the headwaters gave it, was the one which to him best meant the whole. The name Concha used for it. The hut he had lived in with Concha hadn't been far from here, when he'd been a young sprout. A doll, a kind of toy, a live toy who could love you and keep house and laugh and make you laugh. He wanted not to think of her, but could not stop the sequence, first of Concha in those good months and then of how she screamed and wept when El Nopo, that bandit bastard, and the troops of his private revolution came through and took her along with them. You were a young Gringo and you worked for the oil company. You were a Gringo and strong and wonderful, and you were supposed to be able to cope with anything, and you stood there looking into the rifle barrels while they tied your girl to a saddle.

That was what started off the first big drunk. He quit his job clearing trail and got really in Dutch with the company. That was the start of a lot, he guessed. He certainly had stayed drunk a long time.

He opened the valise and got out the bottles. They were fair prey, and maybe, if he got out of here, he could use the clothing, but the papers belonged to Tolling. Some of them were handwritten letters. They ought to be sent home. Holding one of the bottles, thinking of that, he really thought out and faced the first fact. In the end of the dry season as it was now, with the bush at its driest and openest, you could figure on a couple of healthy men taking ten days to go forty miles, if they didn't hit a made trail farther down the river and if they were green at bush travel. You could figure even on two weeks. But you could not figure on three. He knew where he was, as he had told them, about five miles below El Salto, the first fall, and forty miles above Ocantán. At Ocantán there were a Swiss and a number of Mexicans, and at least two double canoes with outboard motors. They would have been here by now; the river was low and mild. Being completely green, the young men had not gotten out. There was only one answer to that one, they were dead by now. Easy enough to happen, too. So here he was.

He opened the bottle slowly and smelled of it. Then he lit the cigarette. Boy, this was life. A remark he had heard somewhere came to mind: "James, serve the champagne in tin cups, the gentlemen wish to rough it." He took a pull at the bottle. It was really prime stuff. He had smoked little the last few days, because the smoke tasted foul, but now his cigarette was good. He meditated taking a swig of water, but decided in favor of letting the liquor glow in his mouth and throat and stomach. He set the bottle down with care and smoked, looking out.

The old Chacaljá — a few miles above here he had lived with Concha, when he was a young sprout full of beans and had a regular job. If you could go there now, you probably could not find the spot, any more than you would be able to find any trace of this camp a few years from now. How long ago was that? He had to do a little counting to figure that this was nineteen fifty, not forty-nine. Usually a little thing like that made no difference. He came out in nineteen hundred, the leap year when it didn't leap, the turn of the century. He liked to say, after the lapse of time had made it impressive, "I came out here at the turn of the century, when I was a young sprout," so that back when he was hardly fifty the Americans had taken to calling him Old Century. Those two boys, Tolling and McDaniels, had called him "Mr. Century" when they first met him. The cigarette was half gone. He took another good pull at the bottle.

Pretty nearly half a century, and not much to show for it. No sign of that fortune he'd been going to make. He'd had one real friend, Whittaker, and old Whit was long gone. Up this same river, too. He wished old Whit were here now to sit with him and pull at the bottle and watch the day go over the Chacaljá and night come down. It would be a pretty night, with a moon, if it didn't cloud up. There'd been a lot of clouds around lately. Be a hell of a note if the rains started tonight and ruined this binge. Old Whit had said one time, when they were both good and drunk, that it was a pity he, Century, hadn't stayed in school and gotten an education. He'd have been a poet or a philosopher, Whit had said. Funny thing, he'd felt something that way about Whit.

Apart from Whit, he couldn't say he'd had any real friends. Knew a hell of a lot of men of different kinds, yes, liked some of them, been able to work and live with a lot of them, but not friends, not really. First he guessed he was too brash, and then maybe too much of a rum-bum. Besides, the more you live in the bush and along the river, the more you want to be let live inside yourself.

There had been a variety of women, some of whom he remembered sharply, some of whom were mere whorehouse blurs, vague punctuations to drinking, but none of them had lasted. He'd have liked to have had Eufemia last, but Eufemia was a Tehuana, and she ended by going home with a Tehuano man, the way they always do. He guessed his kid was a good Tehuano, speaking Zapotec as his mother tongue. The chief thing he could say for all these years was that he'd never worked hard, not steadily that is, and he'd had a lot of fun.

Or maybe the chief thing was that here he was, sick, old, and crippled, and still alive after three weeks. Most white men would be dead by now. The grub left him wouldn't have lasted ten days. If his leg cleared up he could tough it out indefinitely, even after the rains came if he had to. And the two young men were dead. Apart from his leg there was nothing the matter with him. Of course, he guessed he'd been orating to himself a lot, but anyone does that who lives much alone in the bush. He had a drink to his own mastery of the wild country.

As that drink took hold his mood changed. He thought of the great joke of being hired by those two young fellows and how, to clinch the job, he had artfully let them draw out of him every fool story he had ever heard of gold being found. Anyone knew it was all bunk. He'd seen it proven a dozen times. What a joke on them — and now on him, too.

A curassow, big and black looking, lit on a branch not twenty feet from him. He stiffened and reached for his rifle, almost tasting the meat. The bird flew off again. He swore. He had moved too soon, before it got settled. He looked at the little package of rice and his slivers of hearts of palm, studying the rice for a long time. He looked at the bottles, then out over the river. The higher bank opposite was completely in shadow, and the shadow was mounting rapidly up the trees. With a manner of finality he built up the fire, poured water in the tin can, and set it to boil. He watched it in a sort of blankness until the water bubbled

properly, then with the same manner of finality he poured
in the last of his rice and added salt. He cut the hearts of
palm carefully into small pieces and added them. The extravagance which wiped out his entire larder was committed
under compulsion. As soon as the food was in, he drank
again, this time following the drink with a brief chaser of
tepid water. He did not want to empty the canteen and be
forced to the difficult process of going down the bank to the
water. Do that in the morning, on a morning drink.

If only his leg started mending he'd be all right. If he
could get around even as well as he had at first, he wouldn't
worry for grub or for being able to tough it out. He'd last
until he could walk like a man and then, rains or no rains,
he'd get out to Ocantán. They would have made sure he
was dead. He chuckled. It had happened before. Old Century dead and buried a lot of times, and he turns up again.
Just a bad old man, but powerful hard to kill. In one of
the tin cans, underneath bits of newspaper, he still had a
hundred pesos, part of the advance the boys had given him.
He meditated on the simple facilities for pleasure in Ocantán, the known limits of hospitality and the extension of
those limits to be made by the judicious buying of drinks
all round, and he planned himself a pleasant stretch of time
once he got out. The Swiss, Anthaler, set a good table.

The rice was done. The stew lacked meat, but latterly he
had been eating little, both to stretch his small reserve and
because he lacked appetite. Now his stomach had come
magnificently to life under the influence of the whiskey.
The stew was delicious. Cooked, it just about filled the
can. He cleaned it all out, at first greedily, then with more
leisure and appreciation of enjoyment. When there was
nothing left but a few inaccessible grains, with a sense of

lavishness and pleasure he threw the can high. It sailed through the air, turning over on itself, and dropped beyond the bank. He listened for a splash, and was disappointed when he could not hear one. The dinner called for another good slug of Bourbon and the other whole cigarette. He stretched and sighed luxuriously.

Briefly the strong light remained on the treetops across the river, while the wall of the main mass was mysteriously blue; then the light went, and almost without transition the far wall became a black strip rising to the sky while the river itself, which had been dark, acquired reflections of light. Beyond those trees, to his left, he could see indications of the moonrise. Tomorrow would be the full moon. He greeted the night with another drink.

The bottle in his hand brought his mind back to the boys and the plane ride with them. He had been pretty well lost until, just before the engine stopped working, he had recognized El Salto and the S-bend of the river by the big swamp. The swamp it was most likely that had got the boys. Then everything had come unstuck at once, and he hadn't done anything but pray until they pulled him out from under the wing and brought him round. It had been a satisfaction, once he was himself, to tell them instantly just where they were. He remembered now their look of respect, just as he remembered trying to tell them how to get by in the bush, and feeling even then that you couldn't tell it to someone, it had to be learned. You had to live it.

He could not exactly say that his leg had stopped hurting, but he didn't mind it much. He wished he had some coffee to go with his dinner and lead back into the drinks in a proper manner. He wished Whittaker were here. There was mist in the enclosure of air over the river now, and the moon, coming up beyond the ocean of trees, began to reach the upper wisps of it and make them glow. As a result of light at the higher level, the river itself was lost in darkness. It would be nice to have Concha here now, Concha or — he remembered a phrase — or the equivalent thereof. It was MacNamara at Frontera who used to say that. Concha or the equivalent thereof. He could imagine it, but Whit would be better. It would be the end of both bottles, sure enough, if he could turn up again.

Old Century, fifty years in the bush, and what had he to show for it? Lying here like a goddamned sultan, looking at the moonrise over the Chacaljá, with a full belly and a rotting leg, and more of the finest whiskey in the world than he could possibly get down in one night. That was a hell of a note. He held the bottle up to the moonlight to see how far he had lowered it, and as it was not even halfway yet, he drank again.

"Or the equivalent thereof." This stuff had no equivalent. MacNamara, he'd gone back to the States. A lot of them had gone back, some of them had stayed here, dead. Why did they all go back to the States? He could have gone back, two or three times, with a good bit of money in his pants, but each time, like that best of them all, his visit to Mexico City, he got to somewhere where the facilities were good and there he stayed until he was broke. It never made him feel bad, winding up broke. Who the hell wants to go back to the States? Drinking the best whiskey in the world on the moonlit banks of the Chacaljá, when by good rights he ought to be dead a week ago.

It seemed to him that there was some connection between the lowering of the level in the bottle and the lowering line of the shadow around him. He was not able to keep pace,

however, and he did not really try, because to have emptied
the bottle by the time the moonlight reached him would
have been to force his pace unpleasantly and bring pleasure
to an end too soon. It was just one of those fool ideas that
used to amuse Whit. "Don't kill the bottle, just squeeze it
slowly to death." That had been Whit.

He saw the moon, just short of full. He took its light on
his face. The light was a ragged silver line along the edge
of the cut-bank in front of him, and shortly, or he thought
it was shortly, it reached the river. The fact that each change
he was watching was totally familiar did not in the least
decrease his delight in it. As drunk as he was beginning to
be, his appreciation was intensified and he felt, as he had
when he was young, and on other drunken occasions, that
there was much more in this than the eye beheld. Although
familiar it was unique, it was a manifestation of something
great which hovered just beyond the line of comprehension.

The thin mists lay between him and the moon, forming
streaks of luminosity. The jungle on the other side was a
jagged silhouette of deepest blue-black with silver edges and
curious sprays and spurts of silver, or of white, ice-cold fire
along the top. The river swirled black designs in the brightness of its reflections, the moonpath broad and flecked,
breaking up at the edges, merging into an area of blackness
on each side. The ice-cold fire lay on his hand; it lay, barred
and mottled with shadow, around him and between him
and the edge of the bank. The thing was enough in itself
— he needed no one, lacked for no company.

He drank slowly but at some length. The liquor now
really did go down like tea. This is what Old Century's
got, he told himself. He's got the Chacaljá River. He's got

this. I got this and I got the bush, and the satisfaction of knowing that even this old and bad off I can stay alive here and have the love of it. This is what I've got and it ain't hay. He put his bottle to his lips, tilting his head well back, and felt insulted and fooled when it ran dry at the second swallow.

He looked at the empty bottle and then at the untouched one. He did not seem anywhere near drunk enough for the amount that had gone down. He hefted the empty bottle, set it down, picked up the full one, and as he did so, feeling the second bottle's weight, the inner realizations which had been working to the surface ever since he saw these two miraculous containers, which he had been holding back and denying since they began gathering days before, came to the top.

There was the simple, central fact of his leg. It didn't only hurt him like fury, it was not only swelling, it smelled. Unable to wash or change his clothes, he had gathered about him a general, ripe, definite smell, but after enough time has gone by, a man ceases to notice his own odor. This was different. He knew perfectly well what it was and what it meant. With food and shelter, still he and his leg had only a few more days to go, days of increasing pain and wretchedness. And he was at the end of gathering food. Right now he had strength and a sense of well-being out of that God-sent bottle, but he could not survive on that. He was through.

It was, of course, quite unnecessary for him to restate all the factors of his situation to himself. He knew the bush, the river, himself, and how men die much too well. He simply admitted their sum and told himself, This is what I've *had*. So now what?

The surface of the river was now entirely covered with a low-lying mist which lay in slight, irregular waves, shining white, with decorations of soft, bluish shadow. From the main body, higher elements detached themselves here and there. This soft brightness gave a new background for the silhouettes of the growths immediately in front of him, a new value to the dark, silver-topped block of the far side. This phenomenon, too, he knew well. He had been looking forward to it. He nodded his head sagely. He would go to the river, he would join the good old Chacaljá.

Slowly, with great seriousness, he peeled the wrapping off the second bottle and loosened the cork. He put the bottle down. A man should leave some kind of word. He had an idea. If he left a message in the first bottle, the chances were fair that even if it was Indians who found it, they would bring it to Ocantán. He opened Tolling's valise once more, and searched in it uncertainly by the moonlight. He found what seemed to be a blank piece he could tear off a sheet, and a pencil. For a long time he pondered and frowned. Finally he wrote, "Sirvase pagar al portador 1 peso. Died drunk and happy. Old Century William Tecumseh Carpenter." He had trouble making the letters. He folded the sheet, and on the outside, on both sides, printed in unsteady letters, "Llevase a don Alberto Anthaler — 1 peso." After a little thought, he added a cross to impress the Indians.

He rolled the paper in a quill, pushed it into the bottle, and watched it unfold. This was about the best he could do to preserve himself for posterity. It would certainly bother Anthaler and the rest as the news spread along the river to know how he came to end up drunk on such elegant liquor, in his predicament. He corked the bottle.

Then he made a cigarette from a piece of newspaper out of the storage can and some of his stubs. He smoked it slowly and gravely, watching the dance of mist strands, the very slow, dreamy, coiling flow of the main body of the mist on the river.

When the cigarette was gone, he took a short drink from the second bottle. Forcing it into a trousers pocket, he got his crutches, and pulled himself erect much more easily than he had expected. Once he was up he was quite steady, which surprised him and gave him a moment of pride. Then he set to the serious business of getting to the edge of the bank, lowering himself to a sitting position, and letting himself down to the water. Anyway, he thought with satisfaction, I don't have to make it back up again.

At the water's edge, the mist reached to a short distance over his head. Around him was a soft, fuzzy, cool gray-whiteness, and above him a soft glow melting toward a defined central brightness where he faced the moon. The water took his bad leg wonderfully, cooling and easing it. He let himself in, supporting himself on his crutches. If anything, it was chilly in the river but the sense of his body's lightness, the feeling of cleanliness, and the complete easing of his leg were sheer delight.

A down tree projected from the bank near him, one end firmly bedded near the shore, the other bobbing and weaving faintly in a slow eddy. He worked his way to it, moving slowly in the supporting, hindering water.

Under his weight the trunk sank lower, so that it was no trick to sit on it and balance with the water up to his waist. He let his crutches float away. The old Chacaljá, he thought, this is what I've got, this is what I've had. The high boot laced on his healthy leg kept the good water from washing about it as it did the other. He wished he'd taken it off, but it was too late for that now. Balancing on the log, he dug out the bottle, hoping the water hadn't got into the liquor. That was one place the river did not belong. He took a solid drink, his face raised toward the soft whiteness which covered him. Faintly here and there he could make out the outline of the black shadow of a tree. It seemed to him that he was experiencing the essence of the river.

He was sitting in the middle of a misty sphere, which in the direction of the moon contained a great, luminous circle with that brightness in the center. I sure as hell wish Whit was here, I wish he could see this. The good old Chacaljá. He felt the whole river, the vastness of it, waiting. The river and all that that term embraced in its true sense. The slow waters were waiting for him, the *lagartos*, the alligators, were waiting for him. Along the banks the countless roots which drew their life from the river waited for him, and so did the big and little fishes, the water grasses, the buzzards, the insects, and all the various and beautiful snakes, the *nauiacas*, the *masacuates*, the *culebras* and the rest. The only people who did not form part of the river, and who therefore did not have sense enough to be waiting for him to join them, were the men who lived along it. They would be curious, perhaps even worried, about his disappearance; the others would know. The graceful animals who drank at the river and who fished in it, the deer, the lions the iguanas, the jaguars, the big, slow-moving *dantas*, would know, the mists, and the days and nights, the bugs darting over the water, the gravels and sands and rocks. He was conscious of them all, and he embraced them.

The sphere with its area of brightness, in which he could see nothing and beyond which he could see everything, contracted and expanded. The moon-spot tended to whirl or else he was whirling. It seemed to him that he had experienced this manifestation before. He took another good, long pull at the bottle, a longer pull than he really wanted, forcing himself, because he did not think that he would get to take many more. Holding the bottle by the neck with its bottom resting on his thigh, he stared at the moon-spot. It was all waiting for him. He knew it all; if Whit were here right now he thought he could explain to him what that thing was you felt in the beautiful moments, that thing that had always been just out of reach when you watched the moonrise or the dawn, and at such times. His hand fell off the bottle, letting it go into the water with a faint gurgle. Slowly, rather majestically, he followed, his eyes closed, his mouth slightly open, slipping gently, almost noiselessly, into the river, in which he drifted limply, without motion of his own.

A Pause in
the Desert

ALONG THIS STRETCH THE HIGHWAY TURNED
almost north, letting the afternoon sun roast the driver's
side of the blue sedan. The black road kept extending itself
ahead, undulating over minor rises, its farthest point evapo-
rating as a black mist in the vibrations of heat haze. This
part of New Mexico, speaking by the book, was not desert.
There was vegetation, there were areas of greenish overtints,
but they failed to provide contrast with the yellowish or
reddish earth. The rock outcrops were brown; under the
force of the sunlight they seemed black. Whatever its correct classification, the country had the quality of howling.
It had the sentient, hostile personality of a desert.

The man, Huggins, drove intently, wanting to get
through and come as soon as possible to where the road
had punctuations, divisions, and places. He had driven
between Los Angeles and Albuquerque twice before, and
rated this the most repulsive stretch of all. His wife, beside
him, younger, agreeably pretty, alert, was affected dif-

ferently. She kept studying the landscape as if she were trying to master it. Mostly she kept her eyes on the far distance, where streaks of red, brown, and yellow with occasional pale greens and washed-out blues, hot yet subdued, led to the semblance of mountains.

The man was acutely conscious of the woman. He watched her with occasional quick side glances, estimating her thoughts. He was disturbed that she was not repelled by this sorry wilderness, as he was. Had she been, he could have developed a little more his role of the experienced traveler, the guide, alleging himself to be unaffected by it, using a faint touch of masculine mockery. It would have been another little addition to the structure of himself he had been erecting, for her and his own sake, in these last four days. Instead, she seemed attracted by it, and that renewed the uneasy feeling of losing hold of her that he had been putting behind him.

He shook his head slightly, remembering the beginning of their marriage, before he was out of uniform. A little thing like this would never have troubled him then. He told himself he was a fool, and to stop worrying, and he glanced at her again. He could not for long forget the hope that by bringing her on this trip he could restore what had been at the beginning; the obverse of his hope was anxiety.

She said, without properly looking at him, "It's frightening, really, but it makes you want to go way out into it and see what's there. I mean, you can't imagine, you feel you have to look."

"You'd find plenty of nothing."

"Not even Indians?"

He visualized where his road map showed the Navajo Reservation border. "Not for a hundred miles or so." As he had done since they crossed the San Gabriel Mountains, he spoke with assurance, the man who knew the country. Then he told her the story about putting green glasses on the burros so they could eat the desert. It struck the right, frontier note, and it pleased her. I'm doing all right, he thought.

His own principal thought demanded expression. "We ought to make Albuquerque in two hours more. Then I'll have fun introducing you to the Southwest Area gang."

She detached her eyes from the distances to answer. "Past time you brought me along, too. You can do with an eye on you. You and your sales conventions."

The trite, affectionate suggestion that he was a dangerous male when on the loose warmed him with a reassurance he constantly craved. He was clearly older than his wife, in another stage of life. His bare head showed a thinness of his fine, brown hair at the crown, and his forehead ran back beyond its original line. He was dressed in a brightly figured shirt with short sleeves and an open throat, and blue slacks of light material. He was not fat, but he had a soft little extra layer under his skin; looking at his face and throat, one would assume a slight roll on his belly. His forearms were round, smooth, and white. Judging by his wrists, he was a small-boned man who used to be lithe. In these last days of driving and getting out to see the sights he had acquired a pink flush on the top of his head, his face, and the backs of his arms and hands. The back of his left arm, after a couple of hours of direct sun since the road had swung northward, had more than a flush; it would be painful later, but he did not know that.

He said, "This *junta*" (he was proud of the Spanish word, the use of which he had picked up the year before) "may mean a lot to us. This is the third time now I've been picked to represent the California area; I'm pretty sure that there's something good in line for me, and of course the big shots will be here. That's where you come in, Dot. I've really got a better half, and I want them to know her."

He spoke sincerely, warmly. She really looked at him, and gave him a smile. Then she lost herself again in the tumbled distances, showing him less than a profile when he looked toward her, her neat ear and the live, gold-brown curl of her hair under the bright bandanna, mostly blue, with which she protected her head from the wind and dust.

He grunted suddenly. "The car's overheating. Look at the gauge."

She turned to see the needle at the red line. "That looks bad."

He slowed down. He read the speedometer, frowned thoughtfully, then he said, "I think there's a sort of a service station just ahead." On the face of it, the statement was improbable. No land could look emptier, less promising of help. Her doubt was plainly visible. "I think it's about a mile further on." The tenths of miles turned slowly on the speedometer. He kept looking from the figures to the road and back again. "There it is. See — where that clump of trees is."

"Nice work."

He concealed his triumph. The bad luck of whatever had happened to the car was his good luck, giving him the opening for the most impressive demonstration of himself as the man, the guide, the ready and experienced traveler, that he could possible have asked for.

After a thoughtful pause she asked, "Why is there a station here, of all places?"

"People get into trouble, like us, or the kids get to yelling for pop. Bet you it changes hands every couple of years."

"Well, I'm glad it's here. You're sure they filled the radiator at Gallup?"

"Yep. I checked."

He was now driving under twenty, and the heat of the outside air, of the roasted metal of the body, and of the engine assailed them with a blanketing fury. As they drew near they could see that the place consisted of a large, one-story building with a metal roof which blazed a painful silver. Its walls, broken on the side toward them by the one high, square ink spot of a window, were made of local stone which camouflaged itself into the desert. There were some small shacks at the back. On the near side stood two big cottonwoods, wonderfully green; on the far side, at a little distance, a cattle-loading pen thrust its platform at the highway. There was no apparent reason for either building or pen, unless the miraculous existence of those trees somehow required that something be placed by them.

Now they could see that two horses were tied to a hitching rack under the trees, and a big, black truck with slat sides, shiny and new, was parked partly in their shade. From the front of the building a long roof carried well out beyond the gas pumps. Along its edge a sign said that this was a garage, a trading post, and the post office of Huesos, New Mexico. Signs on the ground advertised cold pop, ice water, curios, and cabins. From the opposite edge of the highway two roads ran off in a wide, irregular V, the kind of roads made by the frequent passage of wheels in the same track. Their existence was the most unreasonable thing of all. It was impossible to conceive that there was anywhere for them to lead to in the jumbled, color-streaked barrenness

toward which they separately meandered, and yet their presence, plus the signs on the store, stated that somewhere,
somehow, in unimaginable spots beyond sight, in God only
knew what desolate canyons, beside what water holes
guarded by the skeletons of cattle, there lived people, from
whom this enterprise drew a sustenance of trade.

There were several figures, seated in the deepest shade,
by the wall of the establishment. Huggins turned the car
in to park just outside the pumps. As he shut off the engine, he said, "Listen to her boil."

Dot studied the people reposing along the front of the
store, while a tall boy not quite turned man hoisted himself
slowly from a seat on a wooden box and moved toward the
driver's side of the car. The man followed her eyes. "Local
yokels," he said. After a moment he added, "There's a real
Sioux Indian for you. Look at the braids." He pronounced
all the letters in "Sioux," *Sigh-ooks.*

He got out as the boy came to the door. They looked
under the hood together. The boy said he needed a new
fan belt. He said, "Damn. Okay." He told his wife, "Might
as well get out and stretch. How about a coke?"

"You bet." She was still studying the loungers.

The three men by the store front looked at them with
mild, friendly curiosity. The Indian was sitting on the
ground. His face and hands were mahogany-dark. He and
his face were broad. He wore his hair in two braids wrapped
with yellow and blue tape, reaching, as he sat, almost to his
thighs. There was a beaded band around his very large,
floppy black felt hat, which he wore square on his head.
Otherwise his costume was disappointing, cowboy boots
and denim, all of good quality. They had been seeing Indians since Needles, but this was the first with the braids
one had always heard about.

The other two men sat on a bench. One was tall, spare, with very wide, flat shoulders, a seamed face, a lantern jaw, and a humorous mouth. Under his smallish felt hat his hair showed gray. He, too, wore cowboy boots. The other man was slight, worn fine as old silver is worn. His dark face was slender, thoughtful, strong. He had noticeably handsome brown eyes and one of those thin mustaches with the ends drooping well below the corners of his mouth that one sees in Remington's pictures, but his was snow-white. He wore a neat, moderately wide black hat at a good angle. It went well with his white, collarless shirt and black alpaca suit. His black, elastic-sided shoes, small and narrow, were wonderfully old-fashioned. On his shirt, visible under the open coat, was pinned a badge. A sheriff or something, Huggins thought. It was a congregation of old gaffers. At first he had not thought the Indian old, but on second look he saw he was not young, but ageless.

The broad-shouldered man said, "Afternoon, folks. Make yourselves at home."

Huggins, feeling Western, answered, "Howdy."

Yet another man came out of a side door marked GENT's. He was taller than the broad man, and lean. He wore a work shirt, Levi pants like the Indian's but older, a large hat, boots, and spurs. At the moment he was bowed over. In his hands he was holding objects of some sort.

"Look," he said between chuckles. "By heaven, first time I ever knew you could smoke while you was brushin' your teeth." He extended his hands. "Look." In his left hand he held a toothbrush and a set of uppers, between the fingers of his right hand was a cigarette. He put the cigarette in his mouth, took the brush in his right hand, and demonstrated, shaking with laughter. The white men on the bench smiled, the Indian laughed aloud. The lean man straightened with his back to the strangers. By the motion of his hand, he had put the plate back in place. Seen from behind, he gave no indication of age. He simply looked like a horseman, tall, narrow-hipped, and erect now that he was through clowning.

Huggins looked at Dot, registering disgust, and saw that she was delighted. Then the lean man turned around. He raised his hat, saying, "I beg pardon, ma'am. I come out so tickled I couldn't stop. Hope I didn't upset you."

"Oh no. It was so funny."

She pulled off her bandanna and shook her curls. Huggins was astonished, the gesture was so profoundly one of being at home.

The lean man smiled. His smile was good. His eyes were intensely blue, his face was aquiline. She smiled back at him, then at the others. Their eyes received her with appreciation. Huggins said, "I'll get us some cokes." He went into the store.

The broad-shouldered man followed and sold him cokes and cigarettes in a leisurely, friendly, desultory way. He told the storekeeper that they came from Los Angeles and were going to Albuquerque for the Central Supply Company's area sales convention. The storekeeper told him that he'd never been to California but always wanted to go there, and that it was sure hot around here daytimes but it always cooled off at night.

Huggins glanced over the place with its old-fashioned, general-store quality, noting as an oddity the saddles hanging from the wooden ceiling. He took the cokes outside. His wife was sitting on the wooden box, at an angle to the bench. With the Indian sitting facing inward, and the lean man standing at the far end, she and the other three formed a group. As he came to her she was saying, "Do you mind my asking — are you a Sioux Indian?" Like her husband, she pronounced the word as it is spelled.

The Indian said, "Huh?"

The storekeeper, behind Huggins, interjected, "Soo. No, Steve ain't Sioux."

The Indian said, "No Sioux round here. They live up in Dakota. I'm 'Pache."

The lean man looked down at him affectionately. "A murderin', scalpin' Apache."

Huggins glanced at his wife, then at the man they called Steve. Apache was a word full of connotations and wonder. He felt the same discomfort he had known at Grand Canyon when he had been caught out identifying some Hopis as Navajos. It was important for him to be master of this wild country, and that was not easy when before he had always driven straight through, stopping only to eat and sleep.

Steve said, "Just like in the movies."

Dot and the three old men laughed. The storekeeper had sat down on the bench again. Huggins felt ignored. Because they intrigued his wife, these old yokels had become important. He handed her a coke, then, having thought of and discarded the word "gentlemen," he said, "Any of you boys care to join us?"

The storekeeper said, "Thanks, don't use 'em." The others refused vaguely. The rebuff was plain. He had struck a wrong note, as if he had spoken too loudly.

The slender man with the badge spoke in the manner of one who has finally decided to voice something that has been bothering him. "Pappy, if a horse bucks on you, will those teeth stay in place?"

He had a Spanish accent. The pronunciation was not so

marked as was a certain gentleness with which he spoke, as if the alien words had to be handled delicately. The Apache, in contrast, had been heavy in his speech, bearing down on the English.

The lean man pushed back his hat, revealing a forehead that extended to his crown. "I'd been wonderin' about that myself. This mornin' I went out with the boys to pick out these off-color bulls I aim to pass off on Steve here. I was ridin' my *grullo* horse and he busted in two first off. They stayed in fine."

The storekeeper said, "You're too old to be buckin' out horses."

"He wasn't buckin'. It was just early in the mornin' and he felt good. Didn't have a mite of harm in him." The lean man chuckled. "When my oldest boy was seventeen I was watchin' him buck out a bareback at Winslow. He was throwed on the fourth jump and nearly got stomped on. I realized then and there that now I had a boy to be a damn fool for me, I didn't need to be one myself any more. Slim, I need somethin' to wrap this new toothbrush in, to take it home."

The storekeeper jerked his head. "Small sacks behind the counter by the till. Help yourself." The lean man went in.

Dot said thoughtfully, "You call him 'Pappy'? How old is he?"

Slim said, "He ain't so old — seventy-two. You see him ride, you'll know he ain't old. It's just that when that kid he was talkin' of was born — Steve and him and me was punchin' cattle for the Rockin' Three, up in Steve's country — he bragged so on him that we took to callin' him Pappy."

Not so old — seventy-two. The question fluttered in Huggins' mind, he saw it in his wife's face, but neither of them liked to ask it. Steve said, as if he were giving an order, "You guess how old we are." He gestured with his whole hand toward the woman, then toward the others.

She hesitated. The sheriff said in his soft voice, "Go ahead, miss. It's a game always with the Indians, guessing ages."

Steve took off his hat. His hair was iron-gray. The uncovered braids behind his ears were much too thin to justify the thickness or length of the wrapped portion which fell so handsomely to his waist. They were stuffed, then. Huggins saw his wife's mouth twitch as she grasped this incongruous femininity. You had heard that Indians' hair did not turn gray until they were very old. Dot said, slowly, "Well, if your friend — oh — I'll guess seventy."

"Now him, Anastacio." The Indian indicated the sheriff by turning his head and pointing with his lips. The slender man took off his hat. His plentiful white hair, carefully brushed, curled about his ears. He challenged her with smiling eyes.

Pappy came back. "We're guessin' ages," Slim said, "only you're out. We told on you."

Pappy said, "I'll help you out, ma'am. The shameful thing about these poor old crocks is not how old they are, but how young they are, considerin' their condition." At that, Huggins thought, he looked the youngest of the lot, excepting possibly the Indian.

The sheriff was live and alert. He was fine, but he looked as if he had always been fine, and he was not at all withered. For him she guessed seventy-two, and for the storekeeper, sixty-eight.

The Indian pointed to himself. "Sixty-nine," Anastacio said, "I'm seventy-three." Slim said, "You called the turn on me. I'm the baby, sixty-eight."

She laughed. "Not a one of you looks it."

Huggins felt a shock of jealousy. There was a flirtation between her and these four men. She was sparkling, giving her charm for them, and they were responding. He did not understand it, he felt uneasy, and his glibness, his usual, easy approach to any group, seemed to have dried up in him.

"Now we guess you," Steve announced.

Slim licked and lit the cigarette he had just rolled. "That's easy. Sixteen." It *was* a flirtation.

"No, go on, really guess."

Pappy said, "Twenty-four."

Slim said, "Twenty-five, to be different."

The Californian considered his wife. She did not look that young. They were being gallant.

"I'll string along with Pappy," the sheriff said thoughtfully.

Steve studied her. "Twenty-eight." No gallantry there.

"That's right," she said, "twenty-eight."

Next, he thought, they would guess his age, and with that he would cease to be excluded. It would be all right then. His wife was looking out over the desert, then she turned to the lean man. "You are going to sell him bulls, Pa — Mr. — ?"

"Pappy to you, ma'am, Pappy Evans."

"Thank you. I'm Dorothy — Dot — Huggins. Where do you raise cattle around here?" The moment for inclusion, if it had existed, was gone. That was not like Dot.

"I got a little piece over yonder." Like the Indian, he pointed by thrusting his lips toward one of the dim, improbable roads.

"In that — desert?"

"It does look hard around here, don't it? You see where that dark red streak is about ten miles from here? Well it dips there, and there's a strip of good country, grass all year round."

She stared out along the road. "Aren't you lonely there?"

Slim answered for him. "Him nor me. He's got his folks, and we got lots of neighbors; Steve's cousins."

Steve said contemptuously, "Navajoses."

Slim laughed. "It's all Navajo country from here on. They're my main customers. The Apaches don't think too much of them, even if they are related."

Huggins seized a chance to join in. "You say this is Navajo country right here? I thought the reservation was way over west."

"It is, but that don't stop 'em. Matter of fact, they've always been here."

"You mean, they're allowed off the reservation?"

The Apache said heavily, with emphasis, "Inyans are citizens, just like you. We don't have to stay inside no reservation."

His mind was confused with the thought of apology. The sheriff intervened. "You are new to this country?"

Dot answered, a trifle hastily, "I've lived in California all my life." Humiliatingly, he was glad to let that stand for himself, too.

Pappy looked down at her. "Then you never was West before?"

"West?" She digested his meaning. "Oh. No, I never was."

"This is it, or part of it. It ain't all this harsh. If you and Mr. Huggins" — he gave her husband a polite look — "have time to come by the ranch, we'd be glad to have you. It's pretty around there, and the mountains are close."

She looked at Huggins, questioning, wishing. He said,

"We'd like to, thanks. Maybe we can make it on our way back." There were all sorts of reasons why they would be unable to stop.

"You're welcome any time. The road's good in dry weather."

Slim surveyed the group. "You got the assorted Wild West right here. One cattle man, one wild Indian, one wicked Indian trader, and one Spanish sheriff. He's sheriff on account of he's a Republican and a García; that's four aces in this county."

"It's the fast hand," Pappy said. " 'Stacio's really quick."

She was puzzled. "How do you mean?"

Pappy said, "Amigo, enseñela. Go ahead."

The sheriff looked at her mildly. "When I was a boy, my papa worked at Tombstone. Mr. Earp was marshal then, he showed it to me. You must practice all the time. Like this." His delicate hand barely flicked in toward his waistband under the coat and outward again, armed. The gun was big and ugly, blue-black, with the bluing worn off along both sides of the barrel. It lay steady in his light grasp. Then it disappeared as it had appeared. "It is practice, that is all."

Pappy said to the Indian, "We better get started. I got eighteen two-year-olds in the four-mile corral. Pick yours out today. We can take the rest back to pasture with us, and load yours tomorrow." He looked at the black truck. "You can take six easy in that. You got ropes?"

"If I ain't got enough, Slim has."

"That's what I'm here for," Slim said. "You ought to wait a couple of years, Steve. Pappy's just got two new bulls out of Champion Red Royal from Wyomin'. He'll get some real calves out of them."

"I'll come back. We'll be ready for them."

"You and your folks ain't got but about a hundred and fifty head," Pappy said. "How many bulls do you figure on puttin' with 'em?"

"Hundred and eighty now, and we aim for maybe two hundred. We use these bulls two-three years, then sell 'em to other Inyans. Make better stock all over. My father is buyin' registered heifers after the fall sales. Pretty soon, say ten years from now, we'll be raisin' registered breedin' stock altogether. Then you come to 'Paches to buy bulls." There was deep satisfaction in the last statement.

"I aim to keep on improvin' my bunch, too. There's a shortage of good breedin' stock hereabouts, and on over into Arizona. Ten years from now your outfit and mine can trade, maybe."

"That's right." The Apache rose slowly. "Let's go." Erect, he was a heavy, short man, but his hips were narrow, like the others'.

Ten years from now — Steve's father — the horse was just feeling good. Were these men immortal? Huggins felt almost giddy. Dot's face was full of speculations.

Pappy told Steve, "Get your saddle out of the truck."

Suddenly the young woman woke up. "Wait! You haven't guessed Bob's — my husband's — age. Let's see what you can do with him."

The four old men looked at him. He did not at all want what he had so wanted before; he wished that Dot had stayed forgetful. He did not want their scrutiny, or her seeing him through their eyes.

Slim said, "He's kind of hard to figure. Plump, like Steve here. It fools you."

He was plump, but not plump like Steve, not hard, not

ready for the saddle. Under their eyes — yes, and under hers — he knew that he was soft, pale, commonplace. He had thought his full, lightweight California slacks were smart; now they seemed effeminate. He knew that his hips were heavy.

Slim said, "I'll take forty-three."

Anastacio's eyes caught Pappy's, then flickered for an instant toward the young woman. Pappy caught the message. The sheriff said, "I think thirty-seven."

Pappy appeared to consider. "Yeah, close to there. I'll make it thirty-eight."

That was his actual age, but he knew with certainty that both men were underguessing, as they had with Dot, and for her sake, not in gallantry but in a delicacy of consideration. Dot had caught it, too. She was looking away, and what he could see of her cheek was flushed.

The delicacy had passed Steve by. He studied, then said, "Forty-five."

Dot laughed uneasily. "Pappy got it — thirty-eight." He stood foolishly smiling, wordless.

Pappy and Steve went to saddle up. The boy extricated himself from under the hood and said that she was all set. It took Slim time to figure the bill and make change. As they got into the car the two riders came by.

The lean man said, smiling down from the saddle, "Remember, we'll be lookin' for you."

She said, "We'll remember." Again he had nothing to say, nothing to offer but a smile fixed over sheer hatred.

He started the car and let it run for a minute, listening to the engine. "All okay." He let in the gear.

As they gained speed, they came parallel with the two figures on horseback, who followed a trail even dimmer and less reasonable than the two roads. Seventy-two and sixty-nine. Dot's eyes looked past him, fixed on them, until they fell behind. The significant thing was that she said nothing at all.

In a form of pleading, he said, "We'll make Albuquerque a little after five. We can have a drink and a bath, and then we can have a couple of the best of them up to the room for cocktails." He knew she had heard it before, but he had to run on. "Goldbright is a lot of fun, and Tim Loomis from the big office is going to be there. I want you to know him; he's a great guy."

"That will be nice," she said without interest.

The Touch of Greatness

TO DICK WEATHERBEE, HAMMOND WAS THE greatest of men. His admiration began on the first day, before he had even arrived at St. Peter's, when Hammond spoke to him kindly on board the train. From there on it grew, out of reasonable enough materials. Hammond was not only Major Prefect and football captain, he was also first-string catcher, with a deadly peg to second and a batting average of .329. He held the school record for the forward pass, had tied the discus record, and was a good half-miler. He played a fast game of hockey. He stood six feet one and three-quarters inches, weighed one hundred and seventy-eight pounds two ounces. He was born in Philadelphia, September 6, 1919, and planned to enter Harvard. His average mark (the mark sheet was posted monthly) for the first six months of his Sixth Form year, Weatherbee had calculated, was 79.326.

Hammond was a good guy. He always spoke pleasantly to kids, he was friendly with them, and he never soaked them a demerit unless he had to. It wasn't that he was easy or anything like that, only they trusted him. The other First Formers looked up to him, but not even Lansing shared Weatherbee's special feeling.

Dick didn't talk about it. It was all right to say that Hammond was a good guy, or to root hard for him when he came to bat, but you didn't want to sound all wet. There wasn't much that an ordinary kid could do to attract his attention, particularly if you weren't any kind of an athlete. Dick badly wanted the great man to notice him, but he couldn't figure how to go about it. It wasn't until after the Easter vacation that he hit on the idea of an autograph.

Of course it wouldn't do to let on that the only signature he wanted was the Major Prefect's. Anyhow, it might be a good idea to collect autographs, and if he had Hammond's that would be a swell start. Weatherbee got a small notebook and spent several hours fixing it with alphabetical headings, beginning with "Aviators," and so on. He put in a heading "Friends," and another, after some hesitation, "Masters," and when he got to "S," "St. Peter's Men." That was for Hammond, of course. He had it all done when he found he'd left out authors, so he put a heading for them on the odd page at the back, as "Writers." He cleaned up the ink spots and felt it was a good job. When he had it filled, it would be valuable.

He got Lansing and a couple of other fellows to sign up under "Friends." That made it look more real. Then he gathered his nerve to tackle Hammond one day after dinner, when the Major Prefect was going over to the gym to dress for baseball. He didn't have the face to go to Hammond's study, but waited around in the entrance hall. By great good luck, Hammond was alone.

"Hello, Dick," he said.

"Hello, Hammond. Say . . ."

The Major Prefect stopped and smiled. "What is it?"

"Well — look — I'm collecting autographs and if you don't think it's fresh . . ." Weatherbee broke down. Maybe it was fresh.

"You want my autograph?"

"Yes, if you don't mind."

"O.K." The voice was offhand, but Hammond looked pleased.

"I have a book." Weatherbee dug it out and fumbled with it. "Here, on this page."

Hammond took the book and examined it, showing mild amusement. It was a typical kid job. He read off one or two of the headings. Weatherbee was glad he had some other signatures in there already, under "Friends."

"Under 'St. Peter's Men,' eh?"

"Yes."

Hammond took out his pen and wrote.

"There you are. Got a blotter? Better dry it before you shut it. And make it snappy, or you'll be late for baseball."

"Thanks. I'm going right over."

Weatherbee went to his desk in the assembly room. There he allowed himself a minute of staring at the clear, round writing, "C. Browning Hammond," before he put the book away carefully and started for the gym.

Of course you wouldn't expect Hammond to be excited by having a First Former ask for his signature. He'd been kind of amused. Dick had to admit that the book was messy in spots. It hadn't quite worked out the way he'd imagined it would, although he was glad to have that name written there, where he could take it out and look at it from time to time. And anyway, something was bound to turn up in the long course of the spring term.

Then suddenly May was coming to an end and the hot weather starting, and Weatherbee realized that pretty soon Hammond would leave St. Peter's for good. Weatherbee was in just as much of a hurry as anyone else for the summer vacation, but he wished that he could figure out some way to attract Hammond's notice while there was still time.

He wasn't the only one who was startled by June coming up so fast. Eddie Lansing felt it, for different reasons. The School had a manual-training shop with workbenches such as you could never have at home, and he was putting in all his spare time perfecting a model glider. Dick, who had elected printing, used to watch him sometimes. Eddie explained that this wasn't just a toy, it was an invention.

He got the idea from thinking of catapults on warships. Why couldn't a catapult glider be made which could be sent up from level ground? Ever since the loss of the Samoan Clipper he'd been working on a device for dumping gasoline safely. Now he had hold of something really good, so he dropped the other business and went to it. It was difficult, because you couldn't just copy an established type. You had to have more weight in order to make a good projectile, and the balance had to be just right. He and Dick talked about it a lot. Now it was almost June, and still Lansing hadn't been able to begin on the catapult itself. That was going to be a problem; he needed something strong, much stronger than his arm.

On the first Sunday in June, almost at the end of the term, he was just finishing the model glider when Hammond drifted into the shop to pick up a knife he'd left there. He said "Hello, Eddie" in his usual way as he went by. Lansing answered abstractedly. He was holding down the last corner of cloth, waiting for the glue to dry.

Coming back, Hammond paused. "About finished, aren't you?" He looked at it carefully. He was a bug on aviation himself. "What is it?"

"It's a glider." Lansing took his hand away. The glue had set.

"That's a funny fuselage for a glider. Sort of deep, isn't it?"

"Well, you see, it has to be heavy."

Hammond smiled. "Gliders are generally supposed to be as light as possible."

"Well — you see, this is sort of different."

"Oh? What's the idea?"

Lansing squirmed slightly and got red. "Well — you see — you know how they launch planes off battleships with a catapult?"

"Sure."

"Well, I thought maybe you could sort of throw a glider that way, so that it would take off from level ground."

"Catapult glider, eh? It's an idea." Hammond picked up the model and hefted it. It felt easy in his hand. "About as heavy as a wet football. Is it set to go now?"

"Yeah. I call it the projectile glider."

"You going to try it out?"

Lansing had an inspiration. "I dunno. You see, I haven't got the arm for it. I'd like to get someone who really can throw."

Hammond stared at the model. The wings were three feet across, it was a handsome job. The idea might be goofy, or it might work, at least in a model. He could see sending it across the Triangle, a high flight clear over the top of the big oak in the middle. He was hesitant about playing with a little kid's toy, but he had nothing to do, and had been bored idling in the warm afternoon.

"Would you like me to throw it for you?"

"Gee. Yeah, that would be fine."

"All right, come on."

The workshop was in the Schoolhouse, which stood a little more than the length of a football field from Marby, across the Triangle. Standing on the steps, Hammond hefted the glider again. It was sweetly balanced.

"You're supposed to drive it from the tail," Lansing told him.

"Yeah. I get it."

He aimed straight across the Triangle, to one side of the oak. This would be just a test flight, without trying for full distance. He threw with moderate force. The glider didn't mount as rapidly as it should have, and came to earth in a rather steep dive about twenty yards short of Marby's main entrance.

"You need to adjust the ailerons," Hammond said. "Let's see if she's hurt. She certainly can fly, if we get it right."

They walked over rapidly. Lansing didn't run because he was with Hammond, Hammond because he was with a kid. They picked up the model undamaged, and, taking it onto Marby's steps, bent together over the ailerons, discussing just how to set them.

Boys had gathered round the glider when it landed. Others joined them at the steps, most of them wanting to fiddle with it themselves but keeping quiet in Hammond's presence. By the time Weatherbee came drifting along there was quite a crowd; he had to work his way in before he could see the Major Prefect, MacAlpin, and Reynolds, all in close confab with Eddie.

He wished he'd made something interesting like that. He'd been in on the idea from the beginning, he'd had a kind of share in it. He wished Eddie would say something to him about it; if he himself spoke first it would look pushing, even fresh. He didn't really expect Eddie would. It wasn't as if he'd actually helped. But he had had something to do with it. He stood as close as he could, watching with fixed intensity.

Lansing was enjoying his position, but at the same time he had a wistful feeling that the model had ceased to be his. The big boys had taken it over, and he was just tagging along.

Hammond said, "There, that ought to do it."

Rising to his feet, he stepped forward to the edge of the top step. He balanced for a moment on his right foot, with his left arm raised before him. Having the feel of the thing now, he was going to give it a good one.

Weatherbee stood right next to him on his left, looking up. He'd bet Hammond would send it clear over the big oak, and maybe all the way to the Schoolhouse. He was the fellow who could really make it fly. Weatherbee watched the characteristic pursing of the Major Prefect's lips as he drew back his long arm, just as when he went to forward-pass.

Now Hammond's body hid his arm and the model from Weatherbee's view. The kid turned, looking forward, so as to see it the instant it was in flight. Then suddenly a terrific blow smote his head and left eye and he was shut into total darkness, against which masses of small stars like the ones thrown off by sparklers leapt before him. He found himself sitting down, holding his head and feeling dizzy. Hammond stood looking at him in consternation.

"Gee, kid, I didn't know you were there!"

Even in his slowly clearing daze, Weatherbee was aware of Hammond's deep concern.

"I'm sorry. I didn't mean to get in the way."

Someone called, "Say, look where it landed!"

Hammond turned briefly, then told Lansing, "You better go shack it, Eddie. It works all right." He stooped over Weatherbee. "How do you feel?"

The boy got up. His head had stopped swimming and it didn't hurt much. "I'm all right."

Hammond bent over him, putting a hand on his shoulder.

"Feel kind of knocked out, eh? Want to go up to the infirmary?"

"No, I'm all right," Weatherbee said emphatically. He had a clear sense of power, and of being generous.

He did seem all right, now his color came back. He was positively cheerful. A good kid, Hammond thought, a better kid than he'd have expected.

"You got a handkerchief?"

"Yes." Weatherbee pulled it out. It was reasonably clean.

"Well, look. Soak it in the drinking fountain and put it on your eye, see? When it begins to feel warm, soak it again."

"All right."

Hammond repeated, "I'm awfully sorry."

"That's all right. It doesn't hurt."

Weatherbee went to the fountain. The cold handkerchief did help. He was going to have a whale of a shiner, one that would last for days. He was utterly happy. He got bored soaking his eye and went back to the group on the steps. Everyone gave Hammond lots of room for his next throw. Just after that the outside bell rang, warning to get ready for supper.

Weatherbee came into the assembly room about a minute before time for the last bell. Hammond was at the High Desk, watch in hand. Half the school was already seated.

Hammond said, "How's the eye, Dick?"

"O.K., thanks."

Hammond nodded and smiled. Weatherbee floated to his desk and sat there, his hands clasped in front of him, gazing steadily at the greatest of men.

By the Boys
Themselves

THE HEAD DID HIS BEST TO KEEP HIS FINGER
on the workings of the traditions among the boys, which,
quite as much as the formal disciplines of constituted authority, controlled St. Peter's School. He depended upon
his Prefects' meetings, and particularly upon consultations
with the Major Prefect, for it was in them that both systems,
customary and official, came together.

Experience had taught him that his contact would always
be incomplete, for even the most responsive and responsible
of Sixth Formers were still dominated by an ingrained tradition of secrecy, an almost mechanical defense against
adults. When a case of bullying, thieving, or cheating became too much for them to handle, the Prefects would
report it to the Head. He knew that they usually put off
telling him as long as possible, and he had given up pro-
testing at these delays.

Besides, the Head believed that there were many matters
which were better left to the boys themselves. The School
could not formally punish unmanliness, such as tale-bearing

or the serious offense of freshness, but as long as the tone of St. Peter's held, these things were taken care of along established lines.

On certain rare occasions the customary law came into the open with the full weight of authority behind it, and it was one such time, the ritual of "cleansing" Turkey Munroe, which made the most awe-inspiring moment of Weatherbee's first year. Like all the other new boys in the First Form, he had heard tales of this custom, but it was not much discussed and he was quite unprepared for the event itself.

It actually happened in this way. One Sunday afternoon, MacAlpin, who was a Sixth Former and a Prefect, was going to a little-used part of the cellar where he and Reynolds had hidden a copy of *To Have and Have Not,* when he heard a voice issuing from the long wing that ran off under the library.

The voice was saying slowly and with relish, "Here's another for you."

He stopped and listened. There was a loud *smack* and a gasp.

Then he heard, "How do you like that?"

MacAlpin recognized the voice of Turkey Munroe, the Third Form bully. He advanced on tiptoe, with something of a good policeman's satisfaction. The Sixth Form had been laying for Turkey, but up to now they hadn't got anything definite on him. There was another smack and the gasp again, and then MacAlpin came in sight of Munroe, bent over a smaller boy who crouched on the floor. He saw the shoe in Turkey's hand. Above all he saw the expression on his face. MacAlpin didn't quite know what that look meant, but there was something about it that made him at once sick and angry.

Turkey dropped the shoe, straightened up, and turned pale. Somehow, MacAlpin couldn't touch him. He could hardly stand seeing him.

"Get out," he said. "Get the hell out of here."

Turkey went. At the sound of the Prefect's voice the other boy slowly rose. It was young Lansing, of the First Form. His eyes were dry, his lips were set hard, and Mac-Alpin could hear him breathing through his nose.

"You all right, kid?" he asked.

"Yeah, I'm all right."

The Sixth Former bent down, looking at Lansing's face. On a sudden impulse he patted the boy's shoulder. The kid cried then in spite of himself, and they both felt embarrassed.

"It's all right, feller," MacAlpin said. "Get it out of your system. Take it easy."

He walked off and looked vaguely around the cellar, then came back when the choking sounds had stopped.

"Wipe your face. All right, come along."

He led Lansing to the Alley, the corridor between the library and entrance hall, along which a dozen Sixth Formers had their studies, and took him into his room.

"Make yourself at home," MacAlpin said. "There are some magazines. Wait here till I come back." Lansing looked at him gratefully. MacAlpin was an athlete as well as a Prefect, and already the First Former began to feel better about life.

MacAlpin went directly to the Major Prefect's study. Hammond was in and alone. MacAlpin shut the door behind him and then said dramatically, "Brownie, I want a Sixth Form Council."

Hammond registered exaggerated surprise. "What's eating you? Sit down."

"It's that rat Turkey. I caught him pounding the can off young Lansing. He had him in the cellar and I heard him — " The full picture came back; he forgot his drama and simply told what he had seen. "I want him cleansed, Brownie," he concluded. "You don't know — "

"I've kind of got the idea, Mac. Yeah, you sort of put it across. But cleansing — we ought to just report it to the Imperial Whiskers."

Mac shook his head. "You know what he'd do. He'd put Turkey on bounds or something and try to reform him. The Head doesn't know. Turkey's no good, we just don't want to have a skunk like that in the school. If we cleanse him, you know he won't come back next term."

"Well, we could ask the Old Man to fire him."

"Yeah. Sure. And would he?"

Hammond nodded. "I guess not. Well, maybe you're right. We'll see." He rose. "Let's have a look at the kid."

MacAlpin said, "Oke. I've parked him in my study."

Lansing's sense of importance increased when the Major Prefect came in.

"Hello," Hammond said. "Get up, and let's have a look at your backside. Take your pants down. Go ahead."

Lansing did as he was told. Hammond looked, then he turned to MacAlpin and nodded grimly.

"All right," he said to Lansing, "pull 'em up. You're excused from exercise this afternoon. I'll fix it with Mr. Black." He paused, then added in a stern tone, "Now listen to me — keep your trap shut."

Impressed and slightly deflated, Lansing said, "Yes, I will."

"All right, Mac," Hammond said when they were outside, "go over to Grover Hall and tell Bull. Council right after supper tonight, then we'll go see the Head."

The whole Sixth Form gathered in Hammond's study after supper. Lonergan came in with a joke on his lips, and stopped midway of telling it, sinking with an abashed look to a place on the long window seat. By the time all thirty were present, the room was close-packed. The Major Prefect called them to order, spoke of the great seriousness of the matter, and then MacAlpin told his story. After him, Hammond described what he had seen.

Someone suggested that Lansing be sent for, and there were murmurs of agreement. Hammond dissented.

"The way it is," he said, "no one can hang anything on him for tattling. Mac caught Turkey *flagrante delicto*, and then I ordered the kid to show me the damage. He had to do what I said, but he never told anyone anything. If we brought him in here, it might just get around that he squealed, or hid behind the Sixth Form, or something. You know how those little brats are. We've got all the evidence we need right now, and plenty for the Old Man."

Then he stated the arguments for a cleansing. The idea had been present since the Council began, and at the utterance of the word there was a faint stir among the boys. They discussed the matter with extreme seriousness for half an hour, saying much the same things in different ways. They all made it clear that they were considering a grave step which they were reluctant to take unless the case truly demanded it.

Jameson, who had entered St. Peter's in his Third Form year, said, "The only cleansing there was since I've been here, I had the measles. I don't know much about it. But why is it any good just to soap a guy's face and stick his head in a bathtub? Turkey's tough."

Hammond said, "Of course we wouldn't stand for anything like beating someone up or cruelty in this School. I guess if you've never seen a cleansing you wouldn't know. We ask him some questions in here before we wash his face, but the main thing is the general moral effect when I call him out. You'll see. It sticks."

Bull Sanderson, the Minor Prefect, asked, "Are you sure Whiskers will give us permission?"

Faces turned anxiously to Hammond.

"If we vote unanimously he will."

There seemed to be no more discussion. While the Major Prefect called the roll, one could feel the tension in the crowded room. The vote was unanimous. Something like a sigh, a little movement, ran through them all. Hammond rose to his feet.

"That's that," he said. "I'm going to make sure that Lansing keeps quiet. Now you guys, don't go round looking mysterious. You Prefects stick around. As soon as I've seen the Old Man and got his permission, I want you to get word to the Fifth Form to meet here after breakfast tomorrow. Now I'll explain what each of you guys has to do . . ."

When Hammond had finished, they scattered. In the halls they made a point of discussing basketball, next day's lessons, and other such subjects; later, in their rooms, they talked about the coming ritual. It was the supreme demonstration of the Sixth Form's power, and they rehashed the reasons for their decision with grave satisfaction, avoiding any indication of excitement or pleasurable anticipation.

No one below the Fifth Form caught any inkling of what was happening. Lansing said nothing at all. Turkey made a botch of his recitations next day, but that was not unusual enough to arouse any special interest. To most of the school the whole thing came as it did to Weatherbee and the other First Formers.

He went out of the dining hall after dinner, bursting into

talk as he crossed the threshold. He had not noticed how quiet the corridor was. A Sixth Former said, "Shut up, Weatherbee! Move along." Then he saw that the corridor between the dining hall and the assembly room was lined with big boys on both sides, Fifth and Sixth Formers. Masters and those of their wives who had eaten with the School were passing through the lines. The smaller boys were hurried in startled silence into the big room. The Major Prefect stood at the High Desk, hand on the gong, his face set in grimness, surveying the crowd as it came in.

Weatherbee heard a voice behind him, and Hammond's deep "Shut up, Wortmann. Get to your seat." It was ferociously said. Weatherbee began to be frightened.

He looked around when he was at his desk. There were no Sixth Formers save the Major Prefect in the room. The biggest of the Fifth Form stood by the far door, which was closed, and by the windows, shoulders up, legs braced apart. They, too, were alertly watching the crowd, as though they expected someone to try to break away. A guard at the door to the dining room said, "All in," and Hammond answered, "All right." The double doors on that side were closed and two Fifth Formers took up stations in front of them.

Hammond rang the gong. Weatherbee had heard it countless times, had seen Hammond just as he was now; forty minutes earlier, in the same way, he had brought the School to order before they went in to eat, but this was different. The gong rang louder than the great outside bell in the schoolhouse tower. Slowly the Major Prefect's eyes traveled over the rows.

"Samuels! Sit still!" Everyone jumped.

Hammond's eyes still traveled. "McClure! Look to the front!"

He held them breathless, and then for endless seconds

stood facing them, his height and wide shoulders seeming to grow beyond human size.

Weatherbee knew now that this was a cleansing. It was what he had heard about, and he searched his soul for its burden of sins and errors. He didn't dare to look at anyone, although he longed to spot a guilty face that would end his fear.

Hammond said slowly, each word coming out by itself, "There has been bullying going on in this School." He looked about again, then centered his gaze in one spot. "The Sixth Form wants to see" — he paused before he cracked out the name — "*Munroe*, in my study, at once."

The silence closed down once more. Weatherbee heard Turkey's slow steps, and then saw him as he came to the front, walking like someone dazed. You couldn't make much out of his face except that it was pale. He held his head down and he seemed to be plodding. He walked past the desks to the door, which was opened by a Fifth Former, who did not look at him. The door closed immediately behind him.

There was a scuffling sound outside, a snatch of deep, angry words, then nothing. Hammond nodded toward the back of the room and De Carrel, who was next year's football captain, came up and took the desk. The Major Prefect went out.

One or two boys moved, relaxed. Instantly their names were called, and the assembly returned to its painful attention. After a wait beyond all measurement of time, they heard scuffling again, briefly — crossing the Alley from Hammond's study to the lavatory. They went on waiting. Weatherbee squeezed the fingers of his clasped hands against each other in order. He did this over and over again. He had to do something to prevent the crazy impulse to jump up and shout.

Single footsteps crossed the Alley. They went, with a stumble once, across the larger entrance hall and up the stairs. Louder, stronger steps approached. The door of the assembly room was opened, and Hammond came in. He went to the desk, looked around the room once more, then rang the gong and walked out without looking back. The doors were thrown open.

There was no rush of talk. Boys were slow about moving at all. Weatherbee let his breath out quietly. He sat for some seconds before, following the lead of older boys, he rose to leave the room. Everyone was subdued. Someone mentioned Turkey's name, and another said, "Quiet, you fool."

Lansing looked almost frightened as he walked across the hall to his coat locker. Everyone knew that he had been Turkey's special victim. The other First Formers glanced at him respectfully. Then Gore said in an almost casual voice, "Going over to the gym, Eddie?"

Lansing nodded, and they went out together.

Weatherbee got his cap and coat and started for the gym in his turn. On the way Bill Graham caught up with him.

Bill said in a low voice, "That settled Turkey, I guess."

"Yeah." After a few more steps Weatherbee added, "Turkey hash."

"That's right." Bill nodded to himself, and said solemnly, "We don't stand for bullies here."

"Well, he's got his at last. The whole School'll be down on him now."

They walked on, thinking solemnly of St. Peter's high standards, and the judgment that had fallen upon Turkey.

Mr. Skidmore's
Gift

AT THE AGE OF FORTY-FIVE, MR. SKIDMORE was a middling good architectural draftsman beginning to realize that the great dreams of his early days would never come true. He was a bachelor. He earned sixty dollars a week for a large, noisy firm specializing in very modern design, which he disliked. Shortly after his forty-fifth birthday he was walking toward the subway on Morningside Heights, on his way home from a party, and thinking rather drably about his future, for the party had been only pretty good and he was tired. Crossing a street, he was all but run down by an automobile. Afterward he wasn't sure it didn't hit him, although he had no bruise to show for it. He remembered seeing the thing swing round the corner, his frantic leap, and a curious sensation which he described to himself later as sliding feet first through the fourth dimension, though he didn't know just what he meant by that.

He wound up on the curb, feeling extraordinarily weak and shaken considering how common such escapes are in

New York. His immediate need for a drink was emphasized by the bar which faced him, but at the same time he dreaded the subway ride, including the shuttle, which must follow. He took out his money — one dollar and no change. It seemed a case of no drink or no taxi, and he knew there wasn't any liquor at the moment in his apartment.

He rubbed at the dollar bill with his fingers in the faint hope that it might turn out to be two. Not two months before he had found forty cents in a trouser pocket, but such windfalls were rare. Then, suddenly, for no reason, he was perfectly sure that he had two bills in his hand, and he rubbed again, and so there were.

It was delightful, pennies from heaven, the feeling of pure velvet. He had himself two good highballs and rode home in style, his shock and upset almost forgotten. Arriving at his walkup apartment, which had been picked with an architect's eye for good proportions and never adequately furnished, he was cocky. We all expect the bad breaks in this world; the unreasonable good, the little, unimportant bit of luck, restores a longed-for balance. Standing in his living room with his hat on the back of his head, he fished out his remaining quarter and looked at it.

"I'll double this, too," he said.

And he did.

For a moment he was almost sick. He stared at the paired quarters in his hand. Two bits, four bits. Holy Moses, what was this? He tried again. Then he had four quarters. He sat down.

They were identical, all George Washington 1932's, all worn in the same way. They seemed perfectly good. He studied them a long time while fear and excitement blended.

It was characteristic of Mr. Skidmore that he kept a dollar bill in his bureau drawer against emergencies and had not spent it long since. He got it out and it, too, he doubled. Then he knew that what he needed was drinks, so he went around to the neighborhood saloon.

There were only a few men at the bar at that hour. Standing at one corner by himself, he ordered, and paid for, a Scotch-and-soda. Then, without thinking, he doubled it. The act got no attention at the time, but when he was halfway through the second, the bartender asked if he had had two. Mr. Skidmore said casually that yes, he had. The man seemed seriously puzzled. It dawned on Mr. Skidmore that doubling was a faculty to be used with great discretion.

He was a temperate man, but this occasion was so extraordinary that he ordered and paid for several more drinks before he returned to his rooms. He didn't really believe it, it couldn't be, it would disappear shortly, but while it lasted he must make use of it. His eye lit on his one comfortable armchair.

Rather tentatively, he doubled that. When he had arranged the two, the whole business began to take on reality. A frenzy of doubling came over him. He had to hold himself in check and at the same time he was terrified lest this marvelous gift fade away before he made sufficient use of it. Exhaustion finally drove him to his bed, which by this time was one of twins.

In the morning, the various duplicates had not evaporated. He found himself anxious to get out of this place and back to the ordinary, but when it came to putting a nickel in the subway turnstile, thrift conquered and he doubled the nickel. Beating the subway out of a free ride touched a deep chord within him, and he was filled with confidence.

At the office, toiling over the severely functional decoration of a modernistic shoe store, which he considered painfully bleak, his thoughts were occupied with the implications of his gift. The possibilities were tremendous. But then he thought of the frenzy that had seized him the night before and of his mistake in doubling his drink publicly at the bar. He had got away wth that and in his rooms he had held himself within reason, but there must be caution and planning, the technique must be fully mastered.

He began with his finances. Time and again, when he approached the counter of his local bank, he had half expected the cashier to remind him of the miserable condition of his balance and to chide him for extravagance. He decided to clear that up for good. He cashed the whole of his weekly pay check and, going home, quickly ran the sixty dollars up to four hundred and eighty. After a few days had elapsed he deposited most of this, keeping only a few nest-egg tens, which could produce as needed. There was, in fact, no need for him ever to cash a check again, but he decided it would be less conspicuous if he made withdrawals from time to time, while allowing his account to grow into a reserve which would be handy if his gift ran out on him.

His other actions were similarly cautious. His friends, of whom he had a fair number, noted that old Skids seemed to be doing better than formerly. They were mildly amused by his fondness for pairs and sets of things. They saw nothing odd, and it occurred to no one to wonder that his supply of liquor never ran out in the course of an evening.

Even so, he made some slips. Wanting to double his bookcase, for lack of care he doubled all the books in it and had to send in a hurry for a secondhand dealer. He did not quibble over the low price offered, specifying only that it be paid in clean bills. He was unwilling to be responsible for the enormous increase of germs that would go with doubling the dirty ones first offered him.

One hot night when he wanted to serve juleps, he tried to double the supply of ice and got two iceboxes, which made the kitchen rather crowded. He contemplated making another kitchen for it, but his architectural mind was staggered by the effect that that would have on the planning of the rest of the building, so he did nothing about it. The extra equipment seriously disturbed his landlord and was a great source of humor to his friends.

Independent of his salary, he decided he need no longer go on working on an endless succession of flat-fronted, virginal modern stores and offices. He left the big firm for a position under a much less successful architect who was strictly traditional in his design and specialized in the Tudor, which Mr. Skidmore particularly loved. This architect, as a matter of fact, had no great need for another draftsman. Mr. Skidmore offered to work for him very cheap, explaining that he had come into a little money and was doing this mainly for the love of the work. He said that of course if people knew what he was being paid, they would think he was slipping, so he asked the head of the firm to give it out that he was being retained at a much higher figure. His real idea in this request was to account to his friends for his clearly greater prosperity.

Life for Mr. Skidmore began to take on the roominess and satisfaction which he had originally hoped it might have. He liked his work and was valued in his office. He gave money freely to beggars and organ-grinders. He indulged in openhanded hospitality, serving excellent whiskey, good brandy, and sound wine without stint. He took long weekends off. He had plenty of plates, glasses, and flat silver, and he never lacked for electric-light bulbs or fuses.

Only one thing disturbed his tranquillity, a feeling that,

after all, the uses he was making of his gift were pretty small potatoes. He saw the suspicion, publicity, the utter ending of quiet, private life that would result from any spectacular action. Little incidents like the creation of the extra icebox showed how easy a serious blunder could be. Yet never before in his life had he been able to do anything remarkable or unique. Exercise of his gift was a pleasure to him, and he longed to tackle something really interesting. A bolder man, he felt, would do greater things.

He toyed with various ideas. He thought how beneficial it would be if all the parks in the city could be doubled, but he saw that the process would probably cause a disastrous earthquake and would certainly result in an inquiry. So it went with other possibilities.

He lingered longest over a new form of an old half-wish. Rather lonely in his way of life up to now, he had often thought that a brother, perhaps even a twin, would be a delightful addition to his life. Brothers could live together more easily than other men, he believed. There would be mutual understanding and tolerance. So now it occurred to him that he might double himself and explain that a long-lost brother had turned up.

There were a lot of things the matter with this idea. If he were doubled, which of the two would then be he? Who would the other one be, or would he be both of them? He doubled a lot of curious objects, such as cigarette butts, an unwashed plate, a wet cloth, and studied the utter identity of the duplicates. There was a certain horror in the thought of doing this to himself, but even the horror only added to the fascination.

It kept returning to his mind, and finally he began pretending, experimentally, that there was an alter ego in his apartment. He held imaginary discussions with a person who thought just as he did and heartily shared his opinions and prejudices. He imagined walking in and saying "Hello, old man" to a Skidmore sitting at ease in the duplicate armchair by the fireplace. He came to know this fellow and more and more to wish for his companionship. Furthermore, he felt that re-creating himself would be a real act of virtuosity, worthy of his power.

One night he had in a particularly cheerful party of friends and did himself somewhat better than usual on whiskey. They left before midnight, and he experienced, as he often did, a feeling of letdown. His living room seemed too big and the silence was oppressive. He thought how fine it would be to have someone with whom to talk over the evening, to have continuing companionship. Lack of nerve, he told himself, was all that held him back.

He poured out a nightcap and idly doubled and redoubled it. The four glasses on the table irritated him. He could do better than that. He downed one, then a second. He made up his mind. Then, thinking carefully, he doubled himself. He was trembling as he did it; his heart pounded. But the most frightening thing was that nothing happened. Nothing at all.

He drank the third nightcap and sat staring at the fire, deeply disturbed. Seeing the one drink remaining, he was about to double it again, but he held back. Perhaps he had broken the rules; perhaps he couldn't do it any longer. He thought he'd better wait a while; he'd better let the whole thing rest. Besides, he'd had enough to drink. He finished that one and went to bed.

He had plenty of money and plenty of supplies, so for a week he stayed quiet and let his gift lie idle. At the end of the week he was upset by being apparently cut by one of his best friends. The man was getting off a bus as he got on. He looked straight at Mr. Skidmore, who smiled and was about to speak, but his friend went right on by him with a blank face. Two days later Mr. Skidmore ran into him again, this time on the street, and again his friend seemed about to cut him.

Mr. Skidmore said, "Hey, Dave!"

The man turned, puzzled, and stared at him for a moment. Then he said, "Why, it's Skids. I didn't recognize you. How are you? You look thin."

The man's expression was puzzled, and he said "thin" as if it were not really what he meant but the best he could think of at the moment. Mr. Skidmore went home and looked in the mirror. What he saw was thinness not in the sense of loss of fat but of another kind — an effect of having decreased not in size but in substance. In a strange way he was rather hard to see, although he was not transparent.

He went on with his usual routine of subway and office the next day, but it was a nightmare. Whenever he was unable to see himself, he feared lest he might have disappeared, so that he was always running to a mirror to make sure that he was still visible. His behavior aroused much curiosity among the other draftsmen. When he got home, where he could set a mirror up against the wall and watch himself, he realized that he would not leave the house again until this affliction was ended. He holed up, telephoning for such food as he needed, paying for it from a dwindling stock of cash, and encouraging himself with somewhat more than his usual temperate drinking.

Mr. Skidmore continued to diminish. Perhaps what he

had attempted was against the rules. In trying to double himself, he had planned to omit from his double one or two characteristics, including his cowlick, which he disliked. Perhaps he had overlooked the fact that all human beings are incomplete — fractions, really — and that in trying to double less than all of himself he had multiplied one fraction by another. In any case, he approached steadily toward real transparency.

At last he was down to the original nest-egg bottle of Scotch which he had bought months ago, when his power first became clear to him. He hesitated to crack it. Sometime this thing had to be settled, he thought. Either he still could use his gift or he couldn't. It was not improbable that what was ailing him was no more than his failure to give outlet to so great a power. Without special effort, as one performing an act that had become almost mechanical, he willed the bottle to double.

The bottle, the kitchen with its two iceboxes, the whole apartment remained the same. The only change was that in the moment of willing, Mr. Skidmore faded totally away.

John the
Revelator

IN THE ENDLESS, SEESAW RACE FOR MILITARY
superiority between Russia and the Western World the
relative advancement of their computing machines became
the test of who was in the lead. Constant improvement of
instruments of destruction and of the means of delivering
them at enormous speeds, altitudes, and distances demanded
calculations farther and farther beyond human capacity.
Without ever better computers, progress would stop. Each
country's achievements in this line became matters of ever
greater public interest.

In the U.S., the Navy computer, Mark III, which was
unveiled at Harvard in 1950, drew fair public attention.
Two years later it was eclipsed by the Air Force's Mark IV.
By the time Mark V was set up at Chicago, the public began
to be fascinated and somewhat horrified by descriptions of
the "mechanical brains."

The Russians built and maintained their machines in
greater secrecy within their huge, enclosed research center

behind the Urals. The information about them that was given out to the people contained at first, as did the American press stories, a half-humorous element of human interest. Shortly before the U.S. came up with Luke this trend ceased, following an article in *Red Star* rebuking journalists and certain scientists for bourgeois sentimental anthropomorphism in regard to computing machines.

Luke began as Mark VI, but a week before it went into operation a junior officer remarked that Marks were getting monotonous, it was time we had another evangelist. A reporter took up the idea, the public liked it, Public Relations approved it, and the machine became Luke.

Luke seemed at once human and superhuman. Stories about it developed a standard pattern in which, half jokingly, half seriously, with awe which was real and yet kidded itself, the machine was written up as if it lived. At the end the public would always be reminded that after all it was only a machine and could not function unless a human being fed it a problem and turned on the switches.

Back in the forties, the I.B.M. machines in New York had been the first to show signs of "temperament." Luke and the later Marks, enormously more complex, had various troubles which suggested frailties of the human mind and temper. Their operators spoke of resting them after fatiguing calculations, it was said that Mark V became jittery if it was rushed, and that Luke sometimes grew short-tempered and rejected problems.

Technicians were then working on a machine, inevitably called John, which would, it was believed, be the ultimate product in its line. No one could think of any capability that could be added. This project was backed, not by one service, but by the Department of Defense. It was in anticipation of John's completion that the Secretary issued Department of Defense Circular eighty-nine dash twelve, "Anthropomorphic References to Computers." The circular directed that such machines should be referred to only by the neuter pronoun, and forbade a number of expressions which implied that they were human. Persons under the control of the Department who used such expressions would be warned, and if they persisted would receive formal reprimands which would be recorded in their permanent 201 files (Army and Air Force), jackets (Navy), or civil service records.

Not long after eighty-nine dash twelve (classified "Restricted") came out, *Pravda* ran a scorching article on retrogressive deviationist superstitions about computing machines and other products of Marxist scientific genius. Central Intelligence got word that two young mathematicians had been sent to Siberia for speaking of the machine Russia was then building as "Ivan."

John was built and established at U.C.L.A. John had everything. Problems had to be fed to all computers with their Greek and Latin letters and other symbols reduced to a numerical code, which, in turn, had to be reduced from the decimal to the binary system. The double process often took the mathematicians-in-waiting much longer than it took the machines to solve the problem once they had it. John did all this for itself. You could hand the machine a problem set up in figures and symbols. It scanned this with an electronic eye, encoded it in numbers, reduced these to the binary system, and handed out the result for checking, if desired. From the binary sheet it punched its own tape, proceeded to the solution, decoded that and typed it in final form.

John's retention cylinders (eighty-nine dash twelve forbade the use of the term "memory") had tremendous capacity. Within limits, too, the machine could be guided by voice, interpreting limited spoken instructions in a manner believed to be analogous to the response of the neurons and synapses of the human brain to sounds channeled through the auditory system. It worked at record speed, and no one knew what limits there were to the intricacies of the problems it could solve.

Central Intelligence reported that the new Russian machine was in operation, and bade fair to be a rival to John. It seemed that even the Politburo was speaking of it informally as "Ivan." John's advance publicity aroused a certain horror in the general public. An ill-advised P.I.O. put out a story about the similarity of John's processes from "reading" to calculations on a yes-and-no binary basis, to interpretation or "writing," to the supposed processes of human perceptions, thought, and conclusions. The public added this idea to the knowledge that John's capacities far exceeded man's, and began to be seriously alarmed. To allay these fears, stories went out stressing the fact that John was only a machine. It could do nothing without man. "A mechanical brain is not enough," the most effective release ended. "There must be the thing no machine can possess, the human spirit, the divine spark."

A fantastic-science writer assigned to cover John for UP learned that in test runs it had been found that the machine did best if, when not in use, a weak current continued to run through it. The writer drew an analogy with sleep, and went on to a disturbing fantasy about what John might dream. The Department of Defense tried to ban this writer from further access to the machine. This set off one of those rows, so pleasing to the public, in which the high command is caught way off base. The end result was a relaxing of the general feeling about the greatest of all computers.

John was formally christened, like a ship. A chaplain said a prayer. Public Relations arranged that the first person to present a problem to it should be the Rev. Andrew Lethbridge, a pious and much-loved little man famous for his work among delinquent children. Initial use of John in his service was bound to make a good impression upon a nation growing more and more nervous over every aspect of the race in scientific methods of destruction.

Rev. Andrew Lethbridge described himself as an applied sociologist. His problem was in statistics of delinquency, involving deviation from the mean and probable error. Such calculations are ordinarily made by simple quadratics; the capacities of the new machine, however, allowed him to introduce a range of factors, such as number of years of parental schooling and amount spent on clothing in relation to mean annual temperatures, which put his problem quite beyond the scope of human figuring.

As arranged by Public Relations, the little man was presented to John at four-thirty, immediately after the unveiling ceremonies. Commodore Sandeman, who had been military supervisor of its construction, did the honors. He demonstrated John's various capabilities, with Mr. Lethbridge beside him and the cameras making a soothing record of the minister's benignant profile beside the machine. The commodore was especially proud of the voice-control attachment. To show how this operated, he had the first proposition typed for presentation with an error in it. This was fed to John, who encoded it, started work, then stopped abruptly. A red light went on like an angry eye. The commodore stepped to the speaking tube and turned on the switch.

"Correction," he said slowly. "Second line, fourth character, now capital sigma. Correct to capital sigma sub one. Recode."

John spewed out the original sheet, the red light went off, the machinery started again.

The commodore consulted his watch. He introduced Mr. Lethbridge to Lieutenant Weems of the Navy and Captain Massey of the Army, and left him in their charge. The minister fed in the rest of his material. Shortly the answer came out. He sat down at a desk for a preliminary look at it. Weems put the main switch on "rest current," a position to which he and Massey referred, in private, as "sleep." It was after five. The two officers had had a long day. There were four guards in the big room, and Mr. Lethbridge was beyond suspicion. The officers excused themselves and sloped off.

Mr. Lethbridge laid the solution down with a sigh. Whatever the machine might be used for later, the determinations it had just made would give him and his fellows entirely new competence in their fight against wretchedness. He went over to the computer and studied it, standing beside the speaking tube and the shelf on which John handed out its answers. A few dim lights showed inside the cavern full of bright wires. There was a barely audible, humming sound. He could see the nearer retention cylinders turning over very slowly. He thought, he *is* asleep; I wonder if he does dream. Quite naturally, not at all concerned that the guards were watching, he knelt and prayed.

He spoke his improvised prayer in a soft, thoughtful

voice. He prayed for the intentions of the men who would use John, and spoke of the wonder of God's works as shown in this creation of His creatures. He prayed that John might be used only for good, that directly or indirectly, God Himself might guide him. He said that so wonderful a machine should serve to bring man closer to his Maker. At the end he was thinking aloud more than praying:

"Can you give us the ultimate answer? Can you write the equation for God? What is the symbol to represent him? Can you solve man's real problem, so that all these other problems will be forgotten?"

He rose, dusted his knees, and picked up his answer sheet. The guards let him out. When he was gone, one of them said, "That's one for the book. He was praying to it."

"For it, more likely," another said. "Might be a good idea."

The regular attendants, military and civilian, reported at eight-thirty the next morning, followed in a few minutes by Commodore Sandeman with the senior physicist from Los Alamos, bringing the first military problem. These two found the others in a cluster around the answer shelf with two of the guards, examining a piece of paper.

An Air Force captain saluted. "Look at this, sir. He did this in — I mean, it did this while on 'rest current.' "

The commodore took the paper. On it was a strange formula, in which there were three blanks where symbols were clearly required. No one present could make head or tail of it. The senior physicist said that it made him uncomfortable, but he did not know why.

The guards passed on their predecessor's report of Mr. Lethbridge's prayer. No one had approached John after he left. It was noted that the voice control switch had been left on, there was the possibility that Lethbridge had fed in a formula by voice. This was unlikely; there should have been a corresponding punched tape and binary sheet, but there were not. Investigation showed that Lethbridge, barely able to handle the mathematics of the Gaussian Curve, could never have provided propositions of the complexity indicated by the form of the equation.

The mysterious solution was submitted to various people, all of whom were baffled, until it was handed to Rev. Anthony Price, S.J. He may have read it; no one will ever know. Father Price was a theologian, a philosopher, and one of the top four pure mathematicians in the world.

Father Price started work on the equation on a Thursday morning. By Thursday noon he was dead. The sheet of paper was propped up against some books before him. He was slumped in his chair, his head thrown back, and on his face was an expression of absolute bliss. Brother Benildus, his amanuensis, reported that the priest had taken up the problem at ten-fifteen, following breakfast after nine o'clock mass. He had brought in the mail at eleven. Father Price had raised his hand in a signal not to disturb him. At that point he had written nothing on his scratch pad. The brother came in again at twelve to remind him to come to lunch, and found him dead.

On his yellow pad the Jesuit had written six Hebrew characters. Three of these, in his usual neat script, were arranged in a triangle, vaguely in the pattern of the blank spaces in the equation. They were *aleph, lamed,* and *tau.* Then in a sprawl he had written the word "JAH." That was all.

Before this a rumor had leaked out that John had "talked in his sleep." The Jesuit's death broke further through security. It could not be concealed that the death occurred while he was working on something extremely difficult produced by John. In an interview, Brother Benildus insisted that the Father had not died, properly speaking. He had simply left his clay behind him. "He looked as if he had seen the face of God."

The equation and work-sheet were taken by high-ranking courier to a mathematical colleague of Father Price's in Canada. The Canadian studied them for a few minutes, then handed them back to the courier, saying that he thought it would be unwise to read them. He recommended that the sheets be locked away somewhere safe. They were later deposited in Fort Knox.

Ten days after Father Price's death John turned out another document at night. This was a solid mass of Greek capital letters, plainly non-mathematical. A scientist with classical training who was present picked it up. He started, then in a strained voice he began to read aloud in Greek. Commodore Sandeman, who had been summoned, said, "What the hell does that mean?"

"Eh? Oh — 'In the beginning was the Word, and the Word was with God, and the Word was God.' And it goes on to, 'And the light shineth in the darkness, and the darkness comprehendeth it not.' That's repeated four times."

The incident was classified "Top Secret." It precipitated a searching, futile investigation. The feelings of the high command were not eased when, that same day, Luke added a contribution of his own to a problem looking to a vastly improved guided missile. At the end of his solutions he printed numbers which when decoded made another Greek sentence followed by four figures. Translated, the passage read, "Father, forgive them; for they know not what they do. 23:34." The numbers referred to the chapter and verse in St. Luke. News of this was also suppressed, but outsiders became aware of an uneasiness among the personnel dealing with both machines. Rumors ran through the country. Investigators noted that the rumors were sometimes charged with terror, but equally often with great hope.

Great Britain advised the appropriate American authorities of strange behavior on the part of its own latest computer. Curious items of intelligence seeped out of the reservation behind the Urals. Four more scientists had been sent to Siberia, and it was said that a couple had been shot. The commissar who had been in charge of the construction of Ivan looked to be in line for purging. Among the people of Russia, too, strange tales were circulating.

As has been noted, Luke was short-tempered and sometimes rejected problems. One was submitted to him, to determine the height at which the latest refinement of the H-bomb should be exploded for maximum anti-personnel effect. Luke threw this out, and promptly printed a simple mathematical formula: "600 + (3 × 20) + 6." He continued repeating these figures in answer to everything offered him until, in the early afternoon, they threw the switch and left him to cool off. Even among his attendants there were several with enough acquaintance with the Bible to recognize that the figures came from Revelations.

The public still knew nothing of what was going on, although talk was kept alive by odd actions of the old I.B.M. machine, to which anyone could have access. Luke went back to normal work. John, it was noted, solved whatever problems were offered to him, although sometimes he seemed to do so reluctantly. Captain Massey remarked that John had a much sweeter nature than Luke. (Eighty-nine dash twelve was by now virtually a dead letter.)

One day some very distinguished foreigners were invited to see John handle a non-military problem. There was no reason to believe that anything out of line would occur. The problem dealt with the permutations of the 1400 heritable characteristics of the human body and was expected to shed new light on the vexed question of defining a race. The visitors were attended by a Senator, State Department representatives, and the press.

John encoded the problem and set to work, humming and clicking cheerfully. The first page of answers was dropped to the receiving shelf. The geneticists and anthropologists concerned in the matter picked it up and sat down to study it with their mathematical assistants. The second page came out. The opening line completed an equation from page one, then, to the dismay of the officials in charge, once again came a solid Greek text. To make the matter worse, two of the distinguished foreigners were able to read it with ease, even in the unpunctuated, first-century form in which it was typed.

The text began in the thirteenth chapter of Revelations, jumped to the opening of the twenty-first, then continued with entirely new matter, a passionate exhortation to mid-twentieth century mankind, written with all the same literary quality. John turned out altogether three sheets of this text before he returned to the problem and settled down to a long tabulation of the possible combinations of 1400 heritable characteristics with forty-seven and forty-eight chromosomes.

This incident could not be covered up. The papers had it, and they played it for all it was worth. Nor was there any way after that to keep the press from keeping a watch upon John, Luke, and the later Marks. The papers added Greek scholars to their staffs. The Department of Defense also retained Greek scholars, to sit in with the mathematicians when solutions were being received and segregate from properly classifiable material the sermons — or revelations — offered by the machines.

Once John had broken through the wall of secrecy, it was his practice to produce his texts at the beginning of the day, when he was first awakened by switching on full current. Luke appended his to solutions. Marks IV and V proved to be worth no more than routine coverage by the wire services; the texts that they produced were few and generally garbled. One could only say that they were trying.

The Epistles of John and Luke, as they came to be called, and those of the British machine, known to its users simply as Comp, were circulated throughout the accessible world. It also became clearer and clearer that Ivan was acting up.

Various Soviet periodicals and the official radio ran diatribes about neo-primitivistic, sentimentalist-superstitious deviations concerning computers. An unusual number of arrests were made among the ordinary people. Scientists, generals, and officials of the Politburo were holding closed meetings. There were signs that the people were getting out of hand. The Patriarch and several bishops were put under house arrest, and then turned loose, apparently because of popular indignation. It looked as if the Soviet system might be cracking.

The major churches of the Western World agreed that it would be superstition to believe that the Epistles were revealed. Whatever their source, they followed the lines of true doctrine, should be read by the faithful, and could be used in sermons. Certain lesser churches and many laymen were less skeptical. Daily, crowds gathered before the buildings at New Haven and Los Angeles where the machines were housed, praying and waiting. The Russian government was unable to conceal the fact that pilgrimages were being made to the gates of its closed reservation, and that, by one means or another, Ivan's utterances were being transmitted to the pilgrims.

Among those who waited every morning outside John's building was the congregation of the New African Baptist Church, a group known for its singing. It was their regular practice while waiting to see if there would be an Epistle that day, to sing the little-known spiritual:

> What is John a-doing,
> John the Revelator?
> Writing Revelations
> And the Book of the Seven Seas.

By the third day all present were singing with them, and the song spread. Its simple words and impressive tune touched directly upon the feelings of America.

The ferment among the peoples of the divided world had its influence on their leaders. Both the West and East made concessions in the U.N. Assembly. A new reasonableness appeared. Some of the barriers between East and West Germany were removed and a formula was developing for uniting the two halves of Korea. The Atomic Energy Control Committee, which had stayed recessed for four years out of sheer hopelessness, came together again.

The men who were working on the dreadful new weapons were also affected. Lesser machines had developed a nasty way of refusing to solve certain key problems. John, in his great meekness, would solve them, but in doing so he made their authors agonizingly ashamed. The fact was that for some months no one had been able to bring himself to feed into that machine anything which looked to a really deadly form of progress.

John had been in operation a year. His maintenance crew

ran off a routine reading of his memory cylinders, to check on just what he had stored. The reading was made by John himself, who transposed the impulses on the cylinders to tapes, ran these off in binary numbers, and then decoded. Most of what came out was what would be expected from what had gone in, although there were several formulae that could not be interpreted or accounted for. From one cylinder, however, John produced a series of numbers of one and two digits in no intelligible sequence.

Experimentation showed that these were a code for the Russian alphabet, which, like the Hebrew, was not on John's typewriter. He had recorded what read like one side of a series of telephone conversations, biblical in tone, charged with love, and certainly emanating from Ivan, or whatever — or whoever — controlled Ivan. The outstanding quality was a saintly gentleness, yet through that gentleness were expressed searing opinions of what human leaders throughout the world were trying to do. The conversations were also loaded with information about the problems the Russians were working on.

The high command seized upon this information, then with a shock faced the certainty that the other half of these exchanges, equally unreserved, were available in Ivan's memory. This realization completely ruined what had begun as a day of triumph.

Shortly thereafter in Washington was held a most secret meeting of the key leaders of the United States and the British Empire. No secretaries or advisers were present, no notes were taken. Events since John started operating were reviewed, then there was a presentation of the international situation. Russia had been so shaken and had become so reasonable that, if only the Western Powers could end the dead heat in which they had remained with their opponents for the last years, if only they could pull a little ahead, it should be possible to reach solutions of all the major conflicts. Even control and inspection of atomic energy could be assured. Given certain assumptions, which were undoubtedly correct, the means of obtaining that advantage existed.

The toughest military man, the coldest scientist present shrank from that means, but the end was peace and security for a free world. Discussion was long and earnest. At length the President himself summarized that only for the end stated could the action be justified, that it was for this that the machines themselves were striving, and that if they could ensure victory, then it was their duty before God to ensure it. The council voted unanimously to act.

A selected subcommittee proceeded to confer with two famous brain surgeons who had been minutely investigated. These, Commodore Sandeman, and two of the chief technicians who had constructed John, then disappeared for a period of four weeks.

At the end of that time, at ten o'clock one night, the commodore, accompanied by a number of senior officers of the three services, dismissed the guards from John's building. The officers, armed, stood guard. The surgeons and technicians joined Sandeman in John's room, escorted by some high generals, admirals, and scientists.

With a shaking hand Sandeman turned the main switch from "rest" to "off." The faint lights went out, the humming stopped. The technicians laid out instruments, the surgeons rolled up their sleeves and scrubbed.

"You realize, gentlemen," the commodore said, "that after this — this lobotomy, John will run twenty-five per cent slower. And some day we may reach problems," there was pleading in his voice, "that he won't be able to solve."

A general laid a hand on his shoulder. "We realize, Commodore. We know how you feel. Believe me, nobody is happy about this."

The older surgeon said, "May we have the operating lights, please?"

The lights were turned on, the doctors and technicians entered the machine. One technician was weeping, one was swearing softly. Sandeman went to a corner and sat down at a desk, burying his face in his hands.

The next morning Luke blew a fuse. For several days it blew one whenever it was turned on. Thereafter it functioned as a good machine. John solved problems efficiently, it encoded and decoded, but all its operations were a little slower. Central Intelligence picked up a circumstantial account of how several more scientists, being taken to Siberia from the Soviet enclosure, had cried out as they passed through the main gate, "They have killed Ivan! They have cut us off from God!" The story was unreasonable, because there was good evidence that Ivan was running smoothly.

A brooding sorrow and fear crept through the world. From the computers came only the computations demanded of them. The mathematics of weapons construction progressed rapidly. The Atomic Energy Control Committee recessed indefinitely out of sheer hopelessness. The interchange between East and West Germany was cut off. In short order the world was working its way once again to the war that would really be final.

The
Bystander

HE WALKED ALONG THE SIDEWALK THAT followed the north side of Moraine Park, feeling hunger made agreeable by the anticipation of a good meal, the thin but pleasant warmth of the sun, and the other warmth of his pay, the check cashed, the goodly wad of bills in the envelope in his breast pocket. Life looked better than it had in months. Even Moraine Park seemed to have picked up.

The park was a half block of open space, salvaged from the solid crowding of an area of small housing and small shops by a fluke of civic-mindedness. In the middle of it the remnants of a terminal moraine offered a climbing ground for children and an object lesson in geology for classes from the nearer schools. There were a few trees, a moth-eaten hedge around the whole, and inside the hedge a scattering of benches. The walks inside had been graveled, but the gravel had been pretty well absorbed by the yellow-brown, clayey earth. It was a poor place, no more than tolerable when the trees were in leaf, which now they were not. The sidewalk on the north side had never been paved, although paving it was eternally being promised. From time to time it had received reinforcements of gravel and of cinders; it was more black than yellow, crunchy underfoot in places, in places yielding. The last few warm days had taken the frost out of the ground; the sidewalk was damp under the worn soles of his shoes. It was a ratty neighborhood, and he and Babe were sick of it, sick of pretending that sitting on one of those ratty benches and watching ratty children climb on the rocks was entertaining. A few more weeks of steady work and they'd move back to the kind of section they belonged in.

A policeman was walking toward him from the west end of the park, a tall, wide-shouldered man in a navy blue overcoat, making a dark, almost black, angular accent in the wintry light. He strolled with a slight roll to his walk, as patrolmen often do, and swung his stick from side to side. A car slowly passed his figure, headed in the same direction, toward Jenkins. It was a dark green Buick, moving close to the curb at hardly ten miles an hour. It moved so slowly that it caught Jenkins' attention away from plans for the future enough for him to note that a few years ago it would have been a rich man's pride; now it looked passé with its narrow windshield. The car almost stopped at a point somewhat nearer to him than to the policeman, then picked up speed, passing him. He noticed vaguely a sallow-faced man in the right-hand side of the front seat, who looked him over with an expression of hostility, as if the man could read his mind and knew that he, Jenkins, had a good job again, and one that promised to last, and this were an injury to the sallow man.

Jenkins stubbed his toe sharply and nearly fell. He stopped and looked down to see what had tripped him. A brick was imbedded in the ground, one end projecting enough to catch a toe at the moment it was rising from the earth. Perhaps two feet from the brick, toward the hedge on the inside, a glint of light caught his eye. If the brick did not belong where it was, the presence of the other object was genuinely peculiar. He took a hesitant step, sideways, toward it.

Whatever he was thinking was cut off short by the policeman's voice. "What's the matter with you? You drunk?"

Like many ordinary citizens, he had a confidence in the police which turned to strong uneasiness when he thought he might be running foul of them. For a moment he goggled. He did not remember having seen this man before. The policeman was dark, his eyes were deep-set, his nose short, his upper lip and chin long. He looked young, stupid, and pugnacious.

Recovering from the start he had been given, Jenkins said, "God, no. I tripped on that brick. It's dangerous." He thought that he ought to tell him about the other object, but hostility prevented.

The policeman looked at the brick and kicked it tentatively. "Yeah. Well — "

There was an uproar by the northeast corner of the park. A car honked, then braked into a screaming skid, someone shouted, and as they both turned, a man staggered away from in front of the car, threw his arms in the air, dropped to his knees, and slowly fell forward. The policeman went toward the accident on the run; Jenkins stood watching. The car waited until the policeman was close at hand, then it drove off despite his whistling. When he turned to the

victim, the victim rose suddenly, called the officer an adjec-
tived son of a bitch, and began to run. The policeman gave
chase. Jenkins stared after them, amazed by the whole
business yet somehow pleased by it. When they were out
of sight, he remembered, and looked at the ground near his
feet.

He had seen aright. A clip, for a .45 automatic, he was
almost sure, flattened in the middle by some pressure, was
sunk level with the surface of the walk. The clip lay in
fairly dry cinders, but behind it the yellow clay showed
through, and there he saw the marks of a tire, ending just
before the hedge, the track overlapping itself as if a car had
been backed there and turned. There are the darnedest
things on this sidewalk, he thought. He began to frame how
he would tell Babe about it, "That sidewalk was full of the
darnedest things — " The tracks were of a self-sealing tire.
He recognized them because, during his convalescence and
the workless period thereafter, they had bolstered each
other with a detailed planning for the future, although
sometimes the planning's assertions became entirely empty
and the pretense turned painful. They had a sequence,
which in the past week had become vivid — first, the move
back to a decent neighborhood, then a car again, and then,
when savings had mounted, the beginning of a family. The
last item had led to the idea of puncture-proof tires, and
with the diligence of an active man trapped in idleness he
had investigated the matter. These tracks had been made
by the brand of tires they had decided to buy.

He stooped to pick up the clip. He really ought to leave
it there and wait for the cop's return, he knew, but he was
still angry at the man. He would take it to the precinct
station, perhaps, after he had shown it to Babe and dis-

cussed it with her. They might not give a damn about it, but on the other hand it might be one in the eye for that dumb patrolman.

He had been facing east, then had turned toward the south. He did not see or hear the green Buick come around the block again and coast to a stop behind him. The first he knew that anyone was present was when each of his wrists was taken by a hand and a voice said, "Hold it, Jack."

He started back, at first more angry than frightened. The men on either side of him were neatly dressed, their overcoats were new and good, their hats sporty, their scarves vaguely suggestive of evening wear or of the theatrical district. The man on his left was shorter than he, plump and pink-faced, the one on his right was tall and blond. The tall man, whose left hand had slid up, lightly but firmly, to Jenkins' right elbow, showed him a pistol in his right hand, as one might show an identification card. It was smaller than a .45, but plenty large enough. He spoke again, not unpleasantly, to say, "Take it easy, Jack."

The policeman had given him a start, but these men induced a far colder and more durable fright. The plump man said, "You're comin' with us. A man wants to see you." Jenkins stood rigid, and caught himself almost babbling, then he said, "I don't know you. You don't want me. I'm nobody."

The plump man, his grip steady on Jenkins' arm, said, "That ain't up to us. You come along, and if you're all right, the boss will settle it." At the same time, the tall man poked the pistol suggestively against his ribs. There had been Judo, but that was nine years ago, a routine drill forgotten afterward under the pressure of more urgent business. The thought of resistance barely flickered an instant in his mind. He let them turn him about, and then for the first time saw that the Buick had returned, with the malevolent, sallow man still in the front seat, and the rear door left open. As they moved toward it, another car, a new, black Ford, came to a stop behind the Buick.

The plump man let go of his arm and walked toward the Ford. The tall one motioned with his gun. Jenkins got into the back seat of the green car. The tall man got in after him, closed the door, and settled himself, his right hand in his lap, the pistol, smaller than Army issue but no ladies' toy, pointing toward Jenkins. The sallow man, half turned in the front seat, looked at them both with equal ill will. The proportions of the pupils of his eyes were unnatural and the lines of his face, as well as the color of his skin, suggested profound illness. His eyelids flickered constantly. The driver, a large man, glanced briefly at Jenkins and then sat looking ahead, his hands on the wheel, as though it was second nature with him to be always ready to perform whatever might be the next motion in the chain of his duties.

This was the kind of thing that cannot be. The mere violence of interruption in the foreseen, certain, usual sequence of a day, even of a life, left one in a state of shock and incredulity. Jenkins said, "You don't want me. I — I just don't — well, I was just walking by. I'm not mixed up in anything." He had thought of saying "I'm harmless," but could not quite bring himself to it.

The tall man said neutrally, "That's all right, Jack. The boss is a gentleman. Like Pinkie said, if you're all right, you don't have to worry."

Two men, presumably from the Ford, walked to where the clip was lying. The plump man — Pinkie — opened the outer rear door and got in.

"We're takin' this citizen to see the boss," he said, aiming his voice toward the driver. Then, to the tall man, "He'd better get down."

The tall man said, "Yeah. Down you go, Jack."

Jenkins did not understand. He stared. The tall man, holding up the gun steady in his right hand, gestured with his left. "Down, see? On the floor. You got lots of room."

The driver had turned his head, all of them were watching him. There was nothing to do but get down on the floor. The tall man pressed his shoulders with his left hand, until he was reclining, his knees slightly drawn up, his shoulders resting against the door. The position was tolerable but not comfortable. As he assumed it the sallow man snickered and said, "Down, Fido."

The car went into motion. The tall man said, "For Chrissake, Larry, after the way you've screwed things up — "

Pinkie said, with authority, "All right, boys."

There was a radio box attached to the middle of the back of the front seat. Pinkie unhooked the microphone and spoke into it in a low voice, too low to be heard over the slight whine of the car's accelerating engine. The box answered louder and harshly, like a mechanical parrot, "Come in, T six three." The car settled to standard city speed.

Pinkie said, "Buddy is picking up the package and will deliver it, all okay. We have a passenger for Pleasant."

The box answered "Okay," and Pinkie hung up.

Jenkins thought that there should have been a "Roger," or at least the conventional "Over." Their manner of voice communication was sloppy. The car made a turn, then stopped, presumably for a light. They were in traffic. It moved again, and made another turn. He knew that according to the books he should be keeping track of the turns and timing the ride, and that with one thing and another, alertly, he would know where they took him and this would be the first in a series of means by which he would make his escape at length, only he did not see how the first part could be done, and fiction to the contrary notwithstanding, he had no real anticipation of being able to do anything effective in any of the subsequent parts. Through the opposite side window he could see the tops of buildings. They furnished him no landmark he could recognize; they were just more of the monotonous city.

He looked at the men on the back seat. They did not correspond to the types in which they were supposed to be cast; they did not look like men of his world, but still they were ordinary enough, except that in their faces was something intangible, a quality that impressed him as a sort of blankness, the impact of which upon the observer was that these men were not to be fooled with, that deadliness lay ready to their hands as a tool to be used when indicated. Only the man Larry at all met expectation; hophead, he thought, the traditional killer, sent on some mission and responsible for the error of the dropped, empty clip.

The situation was so unreal, so impossible, that active fear had subsided, although it remained as an undertone to his surface feelings and thoughts. This was a mistake, a thing to be straightened out, surely — and it was in the reservation underlying the concept, "surely," that the continuing vibration of fear became audible — it was a puzzle, to be understood and so mastered. If a man had had combat experience it would be a reflex with him to eject and replace an empty clip, and this Larry, poor weed that he seemed now, might well have had that experience. But the emptying of a clip did not fit what he understood about gangsters, who killed quickly, at close range, and as quietly as possible, unless they staged one of their spectacular, broad daylight, tommy gun jobs. Then a car had been backed over the clip — to pick up a body, perhaps? Or a chance, a coincidence? That sidewalk was full of the darnedest things; the light remark passed wryly through his thoughts. Then the sidewalk should also have been full of shells. If he had turned toward the curb instead of toward the hedge, he might have seen them, and a litter of brass shells might have made some impression on that stupid cop's mind, if he had called the cop's attention to them. His thoughts were escaping among if's; he pulled them back. He was in trouble now on account of the clip, that much was for sure — unless possibly the clip was the coincidence, just another useless object thrown away; the children of the poor brought astonishing playthings with them to the park, and there might have been something else, ransom money, loot, in the hedge. In that case he could certainly clear himself. He encouraged the thought, which did not have too much vitality.

The car turned again, slowed, passed through deep shadow and then into artificial light, and stopped. The driver shut off the engine. All four doors were opened almost at once. Pinkie got out. The tall man said, "This is the end of the line, Jack; sorry we can't take you any further."

It occurred to him that at this point he ought to seize an opportunity to break for freedom, but he had no intention of any such folly. Stiffly and awkwardly he got himself up and out the door by which Pinkie was standing. He was in a basement garage. Four cars of various makes were parked there, and there was room for several more. Pinkie turned, the tall man prodded him with the gun and he followed Pinkie, the other two trailing behind the three of them. Pinkie led the way to a metal door, unlocked it, and they followed him inside.

They entered one end of a longish, bare corridor such as one might find in the service section of any apartment house. The walls were pale green, there was a smooth, reddish-brown covering on the floor, and the light came from bulbs in the ceiling. There were two doors in the inner wall of the corridor and another at the far end, and directly facing them the wider, double doors of a self-service elevator. Doors and frames were painted a green slightly darker than the walls. It was the kind of a place that always made him feel, with all he had had to do with their construction, as though here the architect had grown tired and yet felt that some gesture toward decorating even the basement should be made, and hit inevitably on the same green tones and the same treatment of the doors.

Pinkie said, "Okay for now, you two. Stick around."

The big driver and the sallow man turned down the corridor, the big man saying, "Okay, see you in church," the other not speaking. They walked to the door at the far end, their steps creating a faint, echoing ring, and disappeared through the door. Somehow the manner of their going away in the empty place seemed to Jenkins infinitely sad and portentous, the sound of their footsteps was charged with finality, and as the door closed behind them with a single, sharp, defined sound, fear squeezed his heart so that he nearly trembled.

There was a telephone on a narrow shelf beside the door through which they had entered. Pinkie took it up. After a moment he said, "This is Pinkie. I got this citizen we think the boss ought to see." After a pause he said "Yeah,

that's right," and then, "I dunno, we ain't been talkin'."
After another pause he said, "Just me and Swede; I told the
others to stick around." Finally he ended it with "Okay,"
and hung up.

As he turned away from the phone he nodded to the tall
man, who, obviously, was Swede. He said to Jenkins, "The
boss is free; he'll see you pretty quick," then he pushed the
elevator button.

It was so ordinary — the self-service elevator in the basement, the moment's delay after the button was pressed
down, then the sound of the doors sliding to, and the hum
and the slight rattling noises as the elevator came down.
He knew it by heart, to the more solid click as the machine
settled itself at their floor and the sigh of the doors opening. The procedure brought back the grasp on the ordinary
with which he padded himself against fear.

The elevator had buttons for only four floors above the
basement, so this was not, then, an apartment house, but
a single residence, equipped with the significant outsized
garage. He wondered with what else it might be equipped.
Pinkie pushed the button for the second floor above.
Thinking of what a gangster's mansion and headquarters
might contain, Jenkins found it ominous that the elevator,
the specifications of which he knew, functioned so perfectly
although it plainly was not new.

They stepped out of the elevator into one of those small,
squarish entrance halls one finds in the swankest apartment
houses, where the machine serves a single tenant on each
floor. The hall possessed, among other things, a carpet, a
large, blue and white porcelain vase in one corner, and
against the right-hand wall a good modern copy of an old
settee with an excellent, full-sized, framed print of "L'Ar-

lésienne" over it. The only thing wrong was that in the door of blond wood facing them there was a peephole like a single eye charged with hostility, secrecy, and fear. Pinkie stepped up to the eye and stared into it as though it would reveal to him a priceless secret. The door opened and he went in, then it closed behind him. If in the basement there had been the lonely ring of footsteps and a door that latched with assertive finality, here there was a burden of silence.

Swede dropped his hat and coat on the settee, and jerked his head for Jenkins to do the same. Then he said, "Take it easy. The boss just wants to get the picture from him first."

Jenkins noticed that that was the first time that the man had spoken to him without calling him "Jack," and read in that a good sign. Then he realized that the gun had not been in evidence for some time, and thinking back, as though it were vital to settle the matter, every least item in what was happening requiring to be mastered if safety were to be achieved, decided that Swede must have pocketed it when they entered the elevator. He no longer needed it, of course, and the implications of that renewed his fear and hopelessness.

The door opened and a young man, standing in it, jerked his head backward and said, "Okay. Bring him in."

Jenkins' emotional state had been undergoing change ever since he stepped out of the car. He still knew that his predicament was incongruous, unreasonable, and hardly credible, but that knowledge was no longer cogent. His feelings, rather, were more as if he had been preparing for his entrance into this room for a long time, just as he had been trained and mentally prepared nine years ago through so many stages for the final, equally incongruous situation of leading a platoon into combat. He had not stopped then to think how strange it was that he, of all people, should be in that place for that purpose, how it refuted the logic of all his life, nor did he worry with such thoughts now. He felt now, as he had not then, trapped, and he was afraid, but he moved and carried himself as if the situation were normal to him.

Now, he knew, the thing would be settled, one way or the other. If he was to get out of this, he would have to be on his toes. He felt alert and watchful, almost stimulated, anxious to get on with it, and had no idea that his fingers were in constant, nervous motion against the stuff of his trousers.

The room was large, light, quietly modern, with broad, single-paned windows facing south and a fireplace without a mantel opposite. The prevailing tone was light gray, the color of the armchairs, the carpet, and, yet lighter, of the walls. There was a large, plain, modern desk by the farthest window. More fine prints, widely spaced, provided accents of color. Besides himself, Swede, and Pinkie, there were three men in the room. One was the young man who had opened the door, and the second was so like him that he knew they must be brothers. Their skins were pink and healthy, their eyes gray, and there was a suggestion of smooth muscles under their clothing, cut sharper and more in the gangster tradition than that of the others. When they moved, they moved like dancers or acrobats. The youth and freshness of these two men combined with their appearance of deadliness and of susceptibility to command made them seem chill and inhuman. They watched him without sign of interest or curiosity; they were simply watching.

The third man, who had been standing by the desk talking to Pinkie, came toward him. This, unquestionably, was the boss. He was of medium height, slender, delicately made, and not young. His head was half bald; the corners of his eyes and mouth showed middle-aged wrinkles. The eyes themselves, hazel, were large, his features were well cut and regular; despite his baldness, he was handsome. He was dressed soberly in an excellent brown suit with a quiet shirt and tie. He seemed a man of some breeding and taste who lived well without overindulgence; meeting him under ordinary circumstances, one would find him charming. Jenkins was aware of this quality, but he was primarily concerned with measuring him, trying to see if he could be read. This was the possible liberator, the judge, the antagonist.

The boss looked him over benignly, then he said, "Hold your hands out to the sides, please — that's enough. All right, boys."

The two brothers searched him. It was a disagreeable experience, not only for the hands about his person but the sense of invasion of privacy. His small belongings were taken out and laid on a low table near one of the windows for anyone to see — his billfold, the envelope of money, the clean handkerchief from his breast pocket and the rather dirty one he carried in his hip pocket, his pen and pencil, small change, doorkey, the pack of cut-rate cigarettes he smoked for economy, a stray broken cigarette, a nail clippers, another pencil branded with the name of a store.

The boss said, "Sit down, please," and gestured toward three comfortable chairs arranged in a quarter circle facing the central window. The brothers moved on either side of him; evidently they had him in charge now, and the others, to whom he was accustomed and whom he had come to think of as human and approachable, were simply onlookers.

He sat down in the middle chair, the brothers in the ones on either side, lounging, relaxed, but neither inert nor inattentive.

He had been trying to observe everything, with the idea of having his battlefield clearly in mind. If sudden need should have arisen, he could probably have moved unhesitatingly to the flush, frameless door at the far end of the room, or to the handsome whiskey decanter on the tray to one side of the fireplace, or to any of the lamps, but if he had been taken out of the room and asked to describe its contents from organized memory he would have done poorly. His mind was whirring rapidly within a kind of daze, a sphere of silence that surrounded it, despite the sounds he heard so clearly.

The window gave on bare trees, and beyond them, an apartment house. Whatever façade it may have offered to the street, the part he saw was thriftily built of yellow brick, an excellent but unornamental building material. The windows, set in metal frames, were well spaced and large; at intervals occurred the convexity of bays. From the windows, and from the space of trees between that building and the one he looked out from, he judged that he was in a good neighborhood. For a moment he held the book-derived thought that just across the way were dozens of people leading secure, sheltered lives, having no idea of what was going on so close to them, and tried to feel the irony of it. It was a secondhand thought, of no practical value, and it failed to move him. The boss was carefully going over his things; that interested him much more, and strengthened the courage of his resentment. He strongly disliked seeing those well-kept, neat hands extracting the contents of his billfold one by one. His annoyance was increased by the fact that on the left hand was a jeweled seal ring too large for good taste.

The boss straightened, walked to the center window, and made himself comfortable, resting his weight on the window ledge, half sitting, half standing. He studied Jenkins again, and Jenkins stiffened, waiting.

"I am sorry to trouble you so, Mr. Jenkins," the boss said, "but we think you may be mixed up in some way in a matter we are interested in." His speech was idiomatic, correctly pronounced, and faintly not native. "Perhaps you can tell us something we need to know. If you please, why did you want to pick up that clip, and how did you know it was there?"

"I stubbed my toe on a brick that was sticking out of the walk, and that made me look down, so I saw the clip. That's all."

"But you wanted it?"

"It was a funny thing to see in a place like that. I was curious, I guess. I thought maybe I'd show it to my wife."

"You were having a consultation with a cop, before his attention was distracted."

Jenkins flushed slightly. He had come to hate that policeman, as if he, by being the kind of man he was, had brought about this predicament. "That cop was coming toward me when I tripped. I've never seen him around before; I think maybe he's new and wanted to make an arrest for his record — you know how they are."

The boss nodded, then glanced inquiringly past the brother on Jenkins' right.

Swede's voice said, "His name's Schumann. He's new."

"Anyway," Jenkins went on, "I tripped, and I stopped to look at what threw me, and then I saw the clip and I was wondering about that, and the next thing I knew the cop was asking me if I was drunk. He's dumb. He was hoping I was. So I showed him the brick and he poked it with his toe, and then all hell broke loose down the street and the cop ran off to see about it. It was funny — " He paused, receiving a new thought. "Maybe you know something about that."

The boss allowed himself a faint smile, then became grave again. "You did not tell the cop about the clip?"

"No."

"Why not? You would think — "

'I didn't like him."

The boss nodded.

It was then that Jenkins fully realized the quality of the man he confronted. His last remark had come out of him unguarded and sincere, and between his speaking and the nod the boss had looked into him, his eyes becoming completely apparent as though, like a great bird, up till then he had kept them filmed and had only at that moment unveiled them. Jenkins had a sense of his thoughts having been instantaneously searched, and of a flash of intimate, oddly warm, mutual communication. The boss nodded and the piercing quality was withdrawn from his gaze; although he did not alter his posture in any degree, he seemed to have relaxed. Jenkins felt his own tension let down and a relief well up in him so great that he dared not indulge it. He reminded himself that he was not yet out on the street and free.

The boss said, "A cigarette, please."

The brother on Jenkins' left got up and crossed to a table in one smooth motion, picked up a glass and silver box, and passed it deferentially to the boss. Jenkins saw in him the tame beast of prey, the servile, beautiful killer.

The boss took a cigarette, then he said, "Will you smoke? Or do you prefer your own?"

Jenkins extended a hand, the box was held within his reach, then a table lighter was flicked and brought to each man in turn. The acts of service were correct, the motions in between swift; seconds after Jenkins had his light, the brother was lounging again in the chair on his left. His guard remained on duty.

The boss said, "What is your business, please?"

"I'm an engineering draftsman."

"That is your pay in that envelope?"

"After taxes and the rest; and I paid out a couple of dollars."

The faded eyes studied his clothing, and Jenkins knew that he was reading the indices there, the good quality suffering from too long wear, the frayed place on his shirt collar, comparing these with his weekly take and taking into consideration, too, beyond doubt, the bargain brand of cigarettes found in his pocket.

"You have been out of work?"

"Yes. Until Monday."

"Who are you working for?"

"McClellan and Braun."

"Ah, yes." The boss regarded the tip of his cigarette for a moment. "You knew what you were looking at as soon as you saw the clip?"

"Yes. I was in the war; I saw plenty of them. Anyone could tell what it was, even squashed like that."

There was an intensification of the boss's interest. "Tell me just how it was lying, how it appeared."

"Well, it was squashed down into the cinders and sort of flattened, where the car had run over it."

"The car?"

"I mean, you could see it had been run over." Danger, there was more danger; he had talked too much.

The boss turned toward where Pinkie was standing. "Buddy must be back by now. Get him on the line, please."

Pinkie picked up one of several telephones on the desk and spoke into it. Jenkins did not know just what there was new to fear, but he was ready to fear anything that did not lead straight to his liberation. He should not have admitted to anything more than the undeniable fact of having noticed the clip itself. You have to play it dumb, he thought, you have to stay dumb until you're clean out of here, and after that, stay dumb for the rest of your life if you want any life.

Pinkie said, "He's on the line." He carried the phone, on a yards-long extension cord, to the boss and held the stand while the boss took the hand part.

"Tell me about it," he said into the machine, "I want the details." He leaned against the window reposefully, listening. Then he said, "He did?" waited, and asked, "You wiped them out?" He waited long enough for a single word in answer, then asked, "Did you notice a brick?" Finally, when he had the answer to that, he said, "I'll want to talk to Larry shortly; see that he stays in. Thank you, that's all."

Jenkins saw that Pinkie was filled with curiosity. It was the way he had figured it while he was in the car — Larry, the sallow hophead, the one who had screwed things up, had not only ejected the clip and left it behind, but he had, insanely, backed his car onto the soft ground. Larry was in trouble. He did not see where this could involve him, but he had so unexpectedly, casually, and terrifyingly been so involved in so much already that now he was all tension again, his mind examining, searching, for the new trap. The telephone was returned to Pinkie, who cradled it and restored it to the desk. The hazel eyes came back to Jenkins. Even more clearly the voice inside himself cried danger, the constriction returned to his vitals, and he tried not to let his raised guard show in his eyes.

"Your brick is confirmed," the boss said. "Now, tell me exactly what you saw, please, everything. You are being helpful." The words intended a soothing deception, and this shocked Jenkins; he found new cause for alarm in finding deceit in this man whom strangely he was beginning to like and admire.

He frowned, enacting an effort of memory. "There was this brick, and maybe a couple of feet from it the clip, and the clip was squashed, the way I said. You could see it had been run over."

"You saw the mark of the tire, then?"

"Well — not exactly. You see, the ground right there was cinders. All you could see was a sort of pressed-down place — concave — that a tire would make but a man couldn't have made it by stepping. I didn't have time to look around much. First the cop jumped me and then your — your men took hold of me."

For a long pause during which Jenkins did not seem able to think at all but only waited, and waiting stretched all his fibres, the boss was silent, considering him.

"I think," he said at last, "that you are an innocent by-stander. I do not like to hurt innocent bystanders. You are capable of forgetting?"

"I certainly am." He did not need to force his sincerity.

"Your wife will want to know what kept you."

"Yes." Was this, also, danger? Could the existence of Babe be a threat to him?

"You are her husband. You can think up a story?"

He forced his mind to concentrate, to function in an ordinary manner, setting aside the consuming, thought-destroying preoccupation with getting away. "I can say that Marronetti — he's the head draftsman — asked me to have a drink with him and talk about the job we're on. It would be like him, and I'd go along, because he's the guy who gives raises — and fires people. Only — "

"Yes?"

"Only, I'd call her up from the bar."

Directing his words toward the entrance end of the room, the boss said, "What time did you pick him up?"

Swede answered, "Twelve-sixteen, exact."

The boss glanced at his wrist watch, flat, white gold on a flexible white gold band that faded into his white, hairless, small wrist under the softly blue French cuff. "It is now eight minutes to one. You might have delayed calling that long?"

"Yes. I could have." Relief could no longer be held back. A wonderful limpness overcame him, and over his whole body appeared a light sweat, so that he wiped his hands secretly on his trousers and started to reach for his handkerchief, then remembered that his handkerchief had not been returned. It was just as well; he hoped that the moisture on his face did not show, that he did not thus betray to these men, his enemies, the greatness of the fear in which they had kept him.

The boss said, "Outside telephone, please." While Pinkie was bringing it, he went on, "If you stopped for a drink, you must have had a drink. Scotch?"

"Please."

"Water — soda — how?"

"On the rocks, I think." Mad, the whole business, this proffered drink and banal question and answer no less mad than every other part.

The telephone came to him. He took it from Pinkie and balanced it on his knee, having as he did so a moment's imagination of the boss imperially dialing while the stand remained in a henchman's hands. He dialed, wishing he could be rid of the attentive eyes and ears that made an ordinary voice and manner of speech sheer dramatic virtuosity. Babe's voice came over the line, and now the juxtaposition that had failed to move him in regard to the neighboring apartment house full of people was so poignant that he had to stop and cough. He told his simple, easy lie, listened, agreed that it might be a good sign, spoke an endearment, and hung up. The brother who had been sitting on his right handed him Scotch on the rocks, generously poured. He took it gladly.

The boss said to the same man, 'Bring Mr. Jenkins his belongings," then, to Jenkins, "You must have some compensation for your inconvenience. Would you have difficulty explaining a hundred dollars suddenly in hand — do you gamble?"

His first impulse was to reject the offer, then it occurred to him that a man such as this would feel easier about him if he accepted money. "I sit in on a game, sometimes, nothing very big. Some of the boys in the office go in for that. It would work."

"Good. Pinkie, a hundred please, mixed, in tens or less, and not too new."

Pinkie walked toward the back of the room, out of sight.

The brother was gathering up the things on the low table. Jenkins' thoughts leaped to the shabby apartment and Babe, and as he raised his glass, some inner, silent mechanism of his brain dredged up and handed to the forepart an item for which it had been searching, perhaps ever since he first saw the clip, perhaps only during the last second. Babe had read aloud a story from the paper — last night? He did not remember — because of an exchange they had had about how, in detective stories, murders always are featured on the front page, while in a big city few of them get more than casual mention in the back. An unidentified man found dead, shot seven times by a .45 pistol, and the conclusion of the police that this was an amateur killing of hate or passion, not gang work, because of the manner of it. The body had been found on the north side, far from Moraine Park. It all came together and he realized, as his glass reached his lips, the import and power and danger of his knowledge. The act of starting to drink was automatic, and with it the raising of his eyes unguarded with knowing and alarm.

The boss's eyes unveiled their full brilliance again, and for a second time the two looked at each other with the intimacy that was almost a union. It was too late to look away or pretend, they both knew beyond disguising. At that moment Pinkie handed the boss a wad of bills. Jenkins lowered the glass until his hand was supported by his knee.

The boss stood up. "I am sorry." Regret was sincere in his voice. "Boys, take care of him, please."

One brother rose from his chair, the other emptied his hands and came over from the table. Each put one hand under his armpit, one over his arm at the elbow, and he rose without effort of his own, the glass falling and spilling on the carpet. He made his mouth come shut, and he opened it to say, "But I'm going to forget — I'm not going to talk — I haven't done anything — "

"I am sorry," the boss said again. "I think you have held some information back, and even if you have not, you have figured out too much. You are still an innocent bystander, but we cannot afford to take chances. It is too bad." He gestured decisively with one hand.

The brothers turned him about and walked him toward the far end of the room. He did not say anything more, he did not try to break away, although he would do that, compulsively and futilely, in the garage. He moved his legs in a nightmare, staring at nothing, unsure if he were he, as Swede moved ahead of them to open the door and Pinkie returned the money to its keeping place.

La Spécialité
de M. Duclos

THE JURISTS OF PARIS WERE SURPRISED WHEN
Maître Béchamil, the famous advocate, undertook the defense of Pierre Duclos. The United States had asked for
Duclos's extradition to the province of Connecticut to be
tried for a homicide that he himself admitted he had committed. His extradition seemed certain. Moreover, Duclos
was an Auvergnat, and Maître Béchamil, a Norman, had
often and openly expressed his dislike for the people of
Auvergne. He detested their accent. He distrusted their
smallness, their darkness, their ferocity. He said that they
were emotional primitives in a country founded upon civili-
zation and pure reason, more Spanish than French, more
Latin than Gallic, and that they used too much garlic.

Maître Béchamil was an effective trial lawyer, a brilliant
legal thinker, a gourmet, and a man of sound common sense.
His taking of the case attracted attention that was further
heightened when he exercised great ingenuity to have the
case put over from the winter to the spring sessions. He

did nothing without cause. The delay was essential, for the whole matter hung upon a proper understanding of the *haute cuisine française*. The later sessions would insure that the presiding judge would be no less a person than the president of the Société Gastronomique des Légistes, that famous organization of jurist-connoisseurs, with two other members of the society as his associates. The winter sessions, Béchamil confided to his client, would be presided over by a man who had been seen — here he lowered his voice — sprinkling vinegar upon *rognons sautés madère*. They shuddered together.

Maître Béchamil had equally good reasons for taking the case to begin with. In the privacy of the advocate's bachelor apartment, Duclos had amply proven that he was a *maître chef*. Above all, his amazing variation upon ordinary *sauce blanche*, which was the very heart of the case, was one of those great innovations that enshrine an artist's name in history. The advocate saw a dramatic and striking defense with good chance of success. He also thought he saw the means of at last winning membership in the Société Gastronomique, which was not only a constellation of gourmets but the controlling inner circle of his profession.

Duclos planned, if he was set free, to proceed immediately to Auvergne, where he would visit his relatives and marry his fiancée. With her and her dowry he would return to Paris and open a restaurant. Maître Béchamil found this plan commendable. He asked how long the master chef would stay in Auvergne. Duclos said about a month. The advocate nodded. Inwardly, he smiled. A month would do nicely, he thought.

The case was heard by the panel of three judges for which Béchamil had hoped. The courtroom was well filled, and the presence of an American attaché testified to the importance of the matter. The prosecution put its case bluntly. The evidence was inescapable. The accused had run a restaurant in Connecticut. One evening he invited a group of his patrons to a dinner. In the course of the meal, for no apparent reason, the accused stabbed one of them, a Mr. Willoughby, through the heart with a carving knife. (The pronunciation of the names Willoughby and Connecticut caused the prosecutor no slight difficulty.) It was not for the present court to find the named Duclos innocent or guilty, but merely to determine, as it could not help but determine, that there existed a sufficient shadow of guilt to require him to return to the suburb or province of Connecticut, where he would receive a fair trial under American law.

When Maître Béchamil rose, the audience felt that his case was already lost. The great advocate surveyed the bench. He shook back the sleeves of his robe and adjusted his cravat. He would not, he said, deny the facts set forth by his learned colleague. His client had indeed stabbed one of his guests and patrons through the heart as he sat at the table. He would, however, show the court that this act had been honorable and completely justified. He would further show that it would be a travesty upon justice to deliver a man who was in effect a hero to the jurisdiction of a people incapable of grasping the principles involved.

"I must give you," he said, "some little idea of the populace of that province of Connecticut, adjoining the metropolis of New-York. I must describe them from the point of view of a *maître de cuisine*, a gastronome, and an artist, such as my client."

He described how these people daily wolfed a hurried

breakfast, sped to New-York by train or automobile, and, after a day of the intensely sustained work characteristic of American energy, hastened home, to arrive exhausted, in time only to numb themselves against their fatigue with an excess of cocktails before approaching the pleasures of the table. From this point, by an interesting transition, he reached the subject of clam chowder.

Maître Béchamil described that bivalve, paler than a mussel, tougher than a scallop, less succulent than an oyster, mere leather when cooked. He described the process of the chowder from the crude salt pork smoking in the pan to the completed dish with spots of grease floating in the milk. The bench was impressed, but it was apparent that the judges were wondering what this description of monstrosities had to do with the case.

"Among these people," he went on, "there is a certain affectation of epicureanism. There is also an affectation of the *cuisine*, with a creditable desire to emulate *la cuisine française*. But the mastery of great art requires generations. Just as that great nation leads all others in questions of the machine, so has it a long way to go before its members have absorbed a true sense of gastronomy. Many among them have formed some palate — enough so that they patronized my client's little restaurant. They have not, however, learned to cook. They may produce their chowders, and they are fairly good with a simple beefsteak, but when they step beyond that point, they err.

"It is impossible to persuade them that very little of anything is enough. If one pinch of sweet basil is good, they think, then two are better. In their cooking they seek to taste not the influence of the ingredients but the ingredients themselves. One of those gentlemen concocting a dish in

his kitchen and finding that the receipt calls for a teaspoonful of dry Sauterne will unhesitatingly substitute for it a
tablespoon of one of their wines of California."

Maître Béchamil paused dramatically. The judges looked
profoundly shocked. Everyone glanced toward the repre-
sentative of the American Embassy, who was staring at his
clasped hands and blushing. Nothing had yet been brought
out to prevent Duclos's extradition, but the atmosphere in
the court was now strongly in his favor.

"Among my client's patrons was that Mr. Willoughby,"
the advocate resumed, "a man blindly pleased with his own
cookery. A man who prided himself upon his omelets, and
yet insisted publicly that oleomargarine was just as good as
butter." His eyes flickered toward the judge on the right,
who was internationally famous for his omelets.

"Now, messieurs, I have set the stage. We approach the
day and hour of the act, an act far more deserving of reward
than of punishment. My client, ever improving his art, discovered an amazing variation upon one of the simplest of
all elements of cookery — white sauce — that elevated it to
a celestial plane. I shall not elaborate, as the court will have
the opportunity to judge for itself the deliciousness of this
compound, a product of the purest essentials of French
cookery, of simplicity, perfect timing, and restraint.

"This sauce, my client realized, would become his chief-
est spécialité de la maison. It would become famous as
sauce blanche Duclos. It assured at last his successful return
to his native land. Launched in Connecticut, then transferred to France, where it belonged, it would be a magnet
to Americans, a source of dollar exchange, an aid to his
country in her restoration of herself under the Marshall
Plan. To introduce this sauce, he invited a select group of

patrons to dinner. Among them was the individual Willoughby, included not for his personal character or for his palate but because of his wealth and position, which dictated even that he be seated upon my client's left.

"The sauce was served with the entrée exactly as it will shortly be served to the court. Everyone exclaimed over it. The guests toasted their host and *sauce blanche Duclos*. They asked for the receipt, but my client only smiled. They tasted, they guessed, but the new elements — the secret — were beyond them.

"Supremely happy, my client went into the kitchen to supervise the final moments of the *pièce de résistance*. This named Willoughby, pretending good-fellowship, followed him. Before my client knew what was happening, the man had stepped quickly to the small stove at which my client prepared his personal creations. There was the saucepan with remnants of *sauce blanche Duclos* in it, and there, on the shelf, were all the ingredients. Willoughby scanned the shelf, chuckled, and returned to the table. Shaken, but ever courtly, my client saw the main course made ready and returned to his seat.

"The individual Willoughby sat at his left, as I have said. He had prepared himself for the feast in the usual manner, with an excess of cocktails. Now he leaned over and in my client's ear he said these terrible words: 'Come to dinner next Wednesday, old boy.' And then he named three names, the secret of *sauce blanche Duclos*, and again he chuckled."

Maître Béchamil was silent long enough to let the full horror of the situation sink in. "My client's years in the Resistance had taught him speed of thought and action. Instantly, as fast as ever in a crisis confronting the Gestapo, he grasped the situation. With heavy hand, this individual would prepare a travesty that from then on he would serve under the name of *sauce blanche Duclos*. Before ever the creation was launched, a counterfeit would be in circulation, its reputation would be destroyed, and not only its creator but the French Republic would have been robbed.

"What could be done? How can knowledge be removed from a mind? There was only one thing to do, and my client did it, knowing full well that thus once more he offered the sacrifice of his life if the good God so willed. The essence of what followed you already know. He miraculously made good his escape. I shall not waste the court's time with details of his voyage to Mexico or of his embarkation from there. Suffice it that, having set foot once more upon the soil of his beloved France, this patriot openly assumed his own name, conscious of the correctness of his position, desiring only his vindication."

Maître Béchamil fell silent. The President of the Court said that it was indeed essential that the court examine this *spécialité de M. Duclos*. A table was wheeled in, bearing cooking equipment and ingredients. M. Duclos stepped forward, bowed to the court, and went to work without speaking.

While he made his preparations, the advocate explained that the entrée consisted simply of slices of breast of chicken, broiled, and seethed in white Burgundy. That the court might be sure what was the contribution of the sauce to the whole, a plate with slices of the meat was passed to them. The judges entertained themselves determining the wine and vintage used.

At a certain point, the little chef took three phials from an envelope and emptied them into his saucepan. He then dropped them into the trash receptacle. The sauce was poured over the warmed meat. The combination was allowed to simmer briefly. Then it was placed on dishes and served, with thin slices of good bread and a well-chosen Graves. As the judges tasted, it could be seen that the effect upon them was electric. It began to seem that Maître Béchamil was winning one of his most unusual and brilliant cases.

The judges withdrew to consider. Maître Béchamil waited calmly. He was sure he had made and sustained all his points. He was confident, too, that no member of the Société Gastronomique could permit the secret of such a sauce to be eliminated from the world. He was inwardly pleased, in addition, because he had obtained possession of the three phials as the table had been wheeled out, and already had identified the contents of one of them.

The judges returned. The President of the Court spoke well of the Marshall Plan, and with deep feeling of the liberation of France. He pointed out that these matters, however, were not on trial in his court. It was the specific act of the defendant, which must be considered in its context. There was a man's inherent right to protect his livelihood. There was the sacredness of art. There were questions of national interest. There was the matter of delivering a man for trial under circumstances such that, with all admiration for American jurisprudence, it must be assumed that true justice would not be done, because of a fundamental conflict of mores and of culture. One must doubt that any court in a land of chowder and oleomargarine could understand the values involved.

"Finally," he said, "the theft of a receipt of this order, aggravated by the incompetence of the thief, is an especially despicable form of larceny. The killing of the thief in the very act is legally identical with, but far more noble than, the shooting of a common burglar as he enters one's window. Extradition is denied."

The courtroom cheered. The American attaché departed furtively. M. Duclos embraced Maître Béchamil. The victory was tremendous.

At eleven o'clock the following morning, the advocate told his staff that he would be absent for several hours on personal business. He then repaired to his apartment, proceeding directly to the kitchen. With precise, delicate motions he laid out the publicly known ingredients of *sauce blanche Duclos*. From a locked drawer he took out the three secret elements, identified by him the night before. The crucial question now was: How much of each?

He did not expect truly to duplicate the sauce. Connoisseur that he was, he knew he was a mediocre cook. Duclos would be a month in Auvergne. Time enough to come so close to the real thing that even the fine palate of the president of the society, after the lapse of a few weeks, would believe that he had indeed duplicated *sauce blanche Duclos* simply from having tasted it once before the trial. Election to the Société Gastronomique would then be certain.

He removed his frock coat, put on a large apron, and went to work. A very little of this, he suspected, rather more of that, and of the third — barely a drop? Or was that merely his timidity? Perhaps, in his greatness, M. Duclos had dared use as much as half a teaspoonful. One must experiment, that was all. This time, one-quarter of a teaspoonful. He worked in complete absorption.

The result was not right. It missed being very good — probably by some indefinable yet disagreeable imbalance of the elements. Béchamil sighed and started again. As he stirred and meditated, lost to the world, he was startled into dropping the spoon with a clatter by the sound of a step behind him and a familiar Auvergnat voice saying, "Good day, Maître Béchamil."

He whirled about. Duclos, who should have been in Auvergne by now, walked toward him. He wore a black suit, a white shirt with stiff collar, and a sober tie. Maître Béchamil noticed that his shoes squeaked slightly. He laid his bowler on a chair, and took from under his arm a case about half a meter long, covered with purplish plush.

"I am on my way to the station," he said. "I just stopped by to show you the bargain I picked up. Look." He opened the case. In it lay a carving knife of fine steel, moderately worn and very sharp. M. Duclos placed the case on the table and took out the knife. "Believe you, monsieur, this is almost the exact duplicate of the fine knife I sacrificed when I eliminated the individual Willoughby."

Maître Béchamil said something vague.

The little man glanced at the articles on the table. "You experiment, Monsieur l'Avocat? You encounter trouble?" The Auvergnat accent was stronger than ever. "Incompetence, I fear. No good cook would think that I ever put that" — he pointed at one ingredient — "in a sauce. I had a phial of it along as a blind. Incompetent."

He smiled. He was dark, small, ferocious, the light in his eyes was primitive, he was more Spanish than French, more Latin than Gallic. He caressed the blade of the knife with the fingers of his left hand. Softly, in that detestable accent, he quoted, " 'The killing of the thief in the very act is legally identical with, but far more noble than . . .' "

Thick on
the Bay

THE TWO BOYS WERE STILL YOUNG ENOUGH
to feel that returning home within the accustomed time
was an imperative, outweighing any adverse circumstance,
and besides, with breakfast six hours behind them, they
were hungry. They had had a sandwich apiece at five-thirty,
as they sat in the blind, but that was hardly even a stop-gap.
Clothing which had barely sufficed before dawn now
weighed heavily, their hip boots radiated heat inward, and
the smell of the marsh inhabited their nostrils.

As they came through the last high line of bay bushes
to a clear view downward to the beach, they stopped.

Tom, the older, said, "Golly!"

Chuck shook his tow head. "Thick."

Inland, on the marsh, the fog had been a wide-circling
haze, thinned to pale blue at the top, brazen where the
sun stood, but allowing a fair range of vision. They had
heard the chorus of lighthouses, Beaver Tail's great siren,
Dutch Island's bell, the high whine from Gull Island and

whoop of Castle Rock, but they had not expected anything as heavy as this, throwing untimely doubt around the permanent fact of homecoming. Colorless, quiet waves came out of smoke which hid everything a few feet offshore. Looking to right and left, they could see for some distance along the beach, but toward the bay there was simply nothing. Dutch Island's deep *dong* came to them across a mile of water, a round noise, big, rolling to their feet, melancholy. A gull screamed. The ferry's familiar, busy whistle at Jamestown dock filled their hidden place with loneliness.

The dory lay just before them, central in their circle of vision. She was known, loved, trusted; they went to her as to a companion perhaps wiser than themselves, and stowed their shooting coats under the stern sheets. On them Tom rested the shotgun — Chuck was too young for a shooting license under Rhode Island law — and their bag, two yellowlegs and a plover. They took off their hip boots and socks damp with sweat. Then they sat on the gunwale.

"I've got a compass," Tom said. "I just brought it along."

He disentangled a minute object, its dial about the size of a nickel, from some string and a wad of tissue paper and held it out. Chuck looked at it approvingly. That was forethought, resource, things that appealed to him. He found his older brother talkative and forgetful, it pleased him when Tom lived up to the specifications of his age.

"Do you know the course?" Chuck asked.

"I guess it's about west to the north end of Dutch Island, and it's just about west by north from there to the Big Dock."

"I dunno about the island, I think it's south of west. Besides, how much does this vary?"

"Two points, I tested it." Tom answered promptly, with satisfaction at his own thoroughness.

"I tell you what," Chuck said, "The Cynthia's anchored just off the bar. Let's see if we can hear her bell."

"All right."

They sat listening. The number of audible noises increased; a land bird, the ferry's whistle growing faint in the distance, the chorus of lighthouses, lap of water by their feet, squawk of seabirds, and a motor somewhere behind them, back on Conanicut Island. Tom wet a finger and held it up.

"Southerly breeze," he said, "what there is of it."

They were quiet again.

"Let's smoke," Tom said.

"I won't want to. My tongue's sore now."

Tom knew that his tongue, too, was pinched, but he was the older, he would not admit failure of this pleasure. He tooks crumbs of grape leaves from a pocket, and made a sort of cigarette with some of the tissue paper. The smoke was biting, but the gesture manly.

"I can't hear her," Chuck said. "Do you think she's moved?"

"Not in this fog. Anyway, we can keep the lighthouse bell on our port." As they rose, Tom could throw away his smoke. "Tell you what, we'll keep west-southwest, then we've got to hit the island, and we can lay another course from there."

"All right."

They stepped the dory's mast and, heaving together, launched her. The water was fresh and delightful about their bare feet; they pushed her further out after she was already well afloat and climbed in, wet nearly to the knees.

Both of them knew that better time could be made, in this light breeze, by rowing, but they considered their vessel a sailing craft; save as an occasional auxiliary, rowing was beneath her dignity. Chuck ran the sail up. Tom put an oar out astern, which would give better steering than the rudder, and enable him to scull if need be. He set the compass on a thwart, and as the sail filled, lifting slightly, trimmed sheet and set the course. He was in command, by virtue of age; the authority was a mere form, but jealously observed, the title of master a prized one.

The little boat ghosted sweetly, with a whisper of water along her strakes. Bubbles overside, a lobster-pot buoy, some eelgrass, showed that they were making progress, otherwise they seemed merely to bob up and down in the middle of nowhere, in a small, white sphere with a luminous place east of the zenith. The fixed, familiar noises, their own creak and rustlings, the distant horns, became background for intense quiet.

Chuck came aft to where he could watch the compass, approving the needle's steadiness. Tom was conscious of his brother, anxious to prove himself before him, knowing the intensity of thought and observation which never stopped within his tow head, judgments against which his fluency of speech broke helplessly.

Chuck took a trick at the helm. With boredom, the fog became less impressive and they talked; undirected remarks on the weather, the shooting, the day's plans, veering by irrelevant associations to the subject of Christy Mathewson. Chuck produced from his memory an amazing list of big league percentages and standings. Tom took the helm again. In their talk, they left many sentences incomplete. After a long pause, one of them would say something predicated upon continuous evolution of the matter at hand, but both followed perfectly.

A new sound brought them to alertness. High, so that they raised their faces as they listened, a whistle shrilled, chains clanked, and there was a rumble of machinery. Tom luffed, Chuck ran forward. They showed eath other, then, not that they had been nervous, but that nervousness was ready in them.

"Steamer," Tom said aloud.

It sounded like a big vessel anchoring, but the noise of the chain was not adequate, and why didn't it run out? Why didn't she blow her horn? He rose to his feet, staring past the masthead. A steamer could come into this anchorage, all right, but she ought to have made an awful racket doing it.

They both saw rocks at the same time, close under their bow, and recognized the steep slope of Dutch Island beyond. On the invisible road a heavy wagon rumbled and maneuvered, with trace chains sounding, magnified by the moisture which carried sound directly against their eardrums as though under water. Somewhere up there an officer blew his whistle again in an order to unseen soldiers. Tom eased the sheet and stood off to northward. He had made a perfect landfall.

They skirted the north end of the island, never seeing more of it than its rocky shore, and took their departure from the wild cherry tree just above high tide line, northeast of the mortar batteries. Tree and shore dropped back out of sight in a few yards of sailing, leaving them alone again. Soon after that they picked up a ship's bell to starboard, and shortly heard a man say, in a State of Maine accent like a gull clanging, "Damn this fog," and another answer, "Oh,

what the hell, thar ain't no steamers nigh on to us here."
That was the *Cynthia N. Baggam*, they could visualize perfectly how she lay, her three masts and the white taffrail
around her poop, but they saw no sign of her. A man
hawked and spat, unconsciously they waited to see if they
could hear it strike the water. The first man said, "Nice
weather for rumrunners."

Tom asked, "Shall we make over to her?"

"No. Just waste time. I guess we're all right."

"Sure."

Chuck took another turn at steering. Slowly, the *Cynthia's*
bell became faint astern; for an interminable time they
heard it, then, finding that they were straining to catch the
next stroke and barely able, knew they had progressed. They
were out in the main part of the bay, the channel. Resuming
the helm, Tom made calculations of tide, changing the
course another point to southward. They sailed and sailed,
out of perspective of time or any measure of distance covered. Talk wore itself out. Tom glanced from sail to compass to overside, Chuck watched the sail and the water to
leeward.

The younger boy jerked his head. "One of Hazard's
pots."

Tom glanced over to the black and yellow buoy. "Yep.
We must be past the middle. Whistle for a breeze."

"Un-unh. We've got some."

Whistling when you're not truly becalmed may kill what
wind there is.

They both turned to windward at the noise of a big
launch, a steady roar of explosions, coming up fast from the
southward. Even while they took it in, it drew near, menac-
ing.

"Whoop," Tom said.

They whooped together, trying to sound like foghorns. The roar of the great motor was too close, loud, overwhelming. Tom yelled *"Look out there, look out!"* for all he was worth, throwing the oar down to leeward and then standing there, feeling himself frozen, helpless, while the dory's nose inched around and he wondered if that had been the right move. Part of his mind recorded that this was a rumrunner going it blind, but identification did not lighten the danger. The sound increased beyond reason, a crepitation of irresistible power which must be right on top of them, and still was out of sight. His voice died in his throat.

Chuck had dived between his legs, he saw Chuck come out with the gun in his hands. Seeing his brother's mouth set and the white, frightened determination of his face, Tom was aware in those hanging seconds how young he was. Two years' difference became an immense responsibility. *I'm master, he must not drown.* Chuck pointed the gun low to the water and fired both barrels. Not till then did Tom catch the idea. His heart stood still and all time waited while he listened to the onrushing motor.

Not giant hands tearing a clipper's mainsail could make a noise like that which assaulted them in answer, a rip, a beating run of high impacts, eclipsing even the motor. All around them, seeming within inches of their ears, the air buzzed and cracked like whips snapping. They threw themselves flat on the bottom of the boat. Tom knew the oar was slipping overboard astern, and he ought to stop it, but he could not. Who would have thought they'd take it that way? Was there no way to tell them, it had been meant only for a signal? The machine gun continued its sustained terror, a matter of seconds, a single burst, then stopped as suddenly as it had started. The boat had swung wide to port, was crossing their bows.

There was another vessel close behind, a different quality of racing motor. As they looked toward each other, this one's gun went into action, but no bullets came their way. A special, brief noise, swallowed in others, was not noted then but remained to come up later, something being struck, shots breaking through wood, and a choked-off cry. It was too short for terrified consciousness to add it then to its overstock.

When their blood began to move again, they understood what they had heard. A rumrunner, in flight, firing in panic at their signal, then a pursuing Coast Guard boat, shooting at the sound of the rumrunner's gun, or perhaps sighting her when she swerved to port. The chase was well past them, but a long minute elapsed before they rose gingerly from the dory's bottom. As they lay, they had been in a state of intense communication which continued when they were up, as if they resumed motion, speech, thought through each other's presence, like men leaning upon one another.

Tom said, "I lost the oar."

Chuck passed him one from forward. He swung the dory's stern with wide sweeps of the blade until the sail filled. Recovering the compass from where it had fallen, he got back on his course. The foghorns were still blowing in their established order; Beaver Tail sounded, Dutch Island's bell rang across the water as though the world were really sane.

The dory crept along again. Holding an oar, watching the little needle were ancient occupations, part of a lifetime which had been lost and now was regained. One had a name, family, personal essence, continuity. No harm had been done. Life still had rules and an orderly procession.

"One of Thompson's boats, I guess," Tom said.

Chuck nodded. Tom kept the oar, no word was said about turns at the helm, an atmosphere of crisis still hung. Neither mentioned the shots which brought on chaos; commendable or idiotic. Chuck's action was a closed subject until in the course of months he himself should declare it open for remembering.

Tom's fright slowly transmuted itself into a shaking excitement. All things not done, impossible to be done, clamored inside him. Just now he did not feel friendly to the smugglers, he hoped the rum-chaser had caught them. The dory crawled while he, leaning forward, tried to create an adequate outlet of action in his mind.

Suppose the dory swung the opposite way, he having analyzed the situation, and he struck the shotgun right into a rumrunner's stomach and killed him, and held them in awe until the chaser caught up. Fantastic circumstances carrying little conviction. . . .

Chuck said in a queer voice, "What's that to windward?"

Tom stared. "I don't see anything." Damn old bootleggers, shoot the man just as he turns a machine gun on me. They tumble back in surprise.

"Look again," his brother told him. "Low down there, can't you see something?"

The dream dissolved before possibilities. He scanned again, carefully. I was afraid and I am afraid, what's the matter with me? "Nope, nothing."

"I guess it's nothing. I thought I saw a barrel or something."

They sailed on. Tom's drama broke down against too

recent reality. Later, he would lie awake at night, trying to be fearless, perfect in action. The calmness of foghorns was infuriating. Tom picked up the gun at his feet and returned it to its place on the coats.

"We're pretty well out of the channel, now," he said. "Give her a little more centerboard."

Water came slowly out from under white, woolly nothingness ahead of them, and faded under it again astern. They were moving, they could see that, but it didn't seem to get them anywhere.

At the sight of a red and white lobster pot they both found tongue.

"That's one of Eldred's."

"Yep. We're getting close in."

"I wonder where we'll hit."

"I dunno. Guess we're way off our course, after — after that."

"It's late, too. Sun's high."

The shore loomed gray, outlying rocks became clear — the Lion's Jaw.

"How's that for navigation?" Tom asked.

"Pretty snappy."

The rocks and the meeting of gray-green, almost luminous water with the shore were plainly visible as he trimmed sheet. Behind the rise of the stones, trees showed pale through the tendrils of fog. They stole along the shore, reaching their father's dock with a manner of secrecy. Chuck jumped out from the bow and made fast. Moving with weary, deliberate, expert motions the two boys unshipped the mast and made snug. Tom brought the coats, gun and dead birds onto the landing.

It was over now. On their own dock, they set their feet

upon security and reason, solid reality once more. Parents, and the inside of their own house were close at hand, seen and foretasted. Words welled up in the older brother, relief, an aggressive outpouring. He would like to be terse about it, as Chuck naturally was, he would like to live up to the super Anglo-Saxon heroes of his books; the talk which insisted upon pouring from him piled boastfulness upon achievement, corroded the substance of things done, but he could not keep silent. He turned from the dory now, after making sure she rode well, consciously portraying a wordless hero, and forthwith began to speak.

"Well, we certainly had an adventure. Gee, those bullets went right past our ears."

Chuck remained eloquently quiet.

"Tell you what, when Mother asks us, we'll say . . . Let's say, first, yep, they shot right at us. They heard us yelling." The matter of the signal was, of course, out of bounds.

Chuck said, "I don't want to tell them anything. Let's don't."

Tom stared at his brother. "What's the matter?"

The younger boy's face was white, and there was the intense look again, the luminous quietness. "Well —"

"It's an adventure, Chuck. They can't blame us."

"Well, I saw — You know when I told you to look to windward?"

"Yes."

"Well, it was on the other side. It was bad enough me seeing it, I didn't want you to see it, too." Chuck's voice faded away.

Deeply concerned, Tom asked, "What?"

"One of the rumrunners, I guess. He must have been

hit when the Coast Guard opened fire and fallen overboard."
Chuck's face was sheet-white, like the time they smoked
one of their father's pipes. "He — he flopped, kind of."

Chuck turned aside and was violently, completely sick.
Tom caught him as he staggered, too close to the edge of
the landing.

"Never mind where it falls," he said. "Steady, Chuck,
lie down."

Chuck shouldn't have seen it, he never should have to
carry that weight. Tom knew how he was, how completely
he would have surrounded what he saw, how deeply it
would go in. It shouldn't have been Chuck.

"Steady, feller. Take it easy."

He flopped — the fisherman's phrase, graphic.

Chuck said, "I feel better now."

He dipped up salt water, gargled, and washed his face.
Then he sat up, leaning against a pile.

"You got to get some more color back," Tom told him.
"You still look sort of funny." He looked around. "I guess
they didn't hear us land, we'll surprise them. Say, we did
some swell dead reckoning, didn't we?" Now that he
wanted a flow of talk, it come out stiffly, but Chuck smiled,
responding to his effort. "I bet they think we're still sitting
over on Conanicut."

Chuck rose. His color had returned. "I'm hungry," he
said.

Tom nodded. "Let's go."

They picked up their things and started along the dock.

"Say, Pa'll be mad at me for losing that oar."

"Don't say anything. Maybe he won't miss it for a while,
and then just think it got lost, somehow."

Tom said, "All right." This was Chuck himself again.

He walked ahead of his brother. "We heard them," he said over his shoulder. "They passed astern of us and we were scared, see?"

They stepped from the planking onto land. He looked at the birds he was carrying, small, graceful, limp now, with dangling necks and eyes filmed over. One of them, the plover, flopped when it went down. Just then he was disgusted with guns, death and all killing. He knew there was a fallacy in it somewhere, but did not try to find it now. Letting himself go with the transient emotion was a relief.

Even a few yards inshore, the fog was thinner. Their house, their door stood up before them. They pushed forward toward shelter.

The Bright
Faces

THE HOTEL LOBBY RAN TO WICKER
furniture and potted plants without flowers. It was clean,
and brown woodwork showed the effects of regular rubbing
down with but little revarnishing. The place was not dark,
but moderately dim, and much cooler than the boardwalk
outside.

A man and two children sat together near a shaded window, narrowly open at the bottom for air. The man sat in
a chair, the children, a boy of about fourteen and a girl of
twelve, sat together, facing him on a settee. The children
seemed sunlit even in the shadows of the lobby. Their
resemblance to the man was apparent, yet the difference
between them and him amounted to oppositeness. The
man himself was aware of it; he was talking easily, holding
their strong interest as he told them how he had come by
the Purple Heart, but all the time he was intensely watchful
and aware. They had their mother's really blond, curly hair,
brilliant and perfect on their young heads. His own hair

133

was dull brown. They had his mother's chin, the firm rounded line, and he remembered the strength, the good-tempered obstinacy that went with it. His own chin was smaller, not quite adequate to his face. The children wore careless, old playclothes. They were deeply tanned, and they looked well cared for. In his seersucker suit he looked at once citified and shabby. As he talked he noted the chins, and watched the gray eyes, wide and fixed upon him with their listening. His hand went up and touched lightly the Purple Heart badge in the lapel of his coat.

When he had seen them last, nearly four years ago, they had not been formed. Even now you could not altogether tell from what ancestral lines they would draw their final, new composite of features. The well-defined likenesses affected him strongly, but more than anything else their brightness, the pellucid, tranquil clarity of their faces pulled at him, so that he wanted to take them in his arms and cry out, "You're mine, you're mine!"

The telling of his war experiences seemed to have bridged the gap of years. He felt that they were in touch again. When he ended the tale of his wound, he sat back, smiling, feeling surer of himself, and lit a cigarette.

With the pomposity of the young, the boy said, "You know, it's swell to know that your dad's a hero." The girl nodded.

He blushed. "Not a hero, feller. Just — well — I just kept up with a gang."

There was a pause. He looked at his wrist watch. Time had gone fast.

The boy said, "Tell us some more about Japan."

He said, "Wait a minute. Your mother will be coming for you shortly, and we have business. Now, the reason I came here was to put an end to all this fooling around. I came here to get you and take you back to my place for a real visit."

The children were astonished. "But, Dad," the boy said, "we wrote you that we can't come. We've got so much to do here."

The man's mouth twitched momentarily, then he recaptured his easy, half-smiling expression.

"Look. The last time I saw you was in 'forty-three, when I had leave before I was shipped, right?"

The children nodded.

"Now, for months I've written you that when my vacation came I wanted you to stay with me, right?"

They nodded again. Their expressions had not changed greatly, their faces were still clear and bright, but the look of interest had gone.

"And didn't you write me, way back, that you were looking forward to seeing me?"

The girl said, "We are seeing you. It's been nice."

"You don't think that an afternoon's visit is enough after four years, do you?"

"You can come again, can't you?"

The man pressed his lips together and looked out the window. How do you make them *feel?*

"Not very easily. You kids — I guess you're used to getting along without me. But I'm your father. I want to have you with me, don't you see?"

The boy considered. "I'm sorry, Dad, but I guess Joan and I are just — well, we're sewed up. We're in the junior races, you know; we can't miss out on those. Joan's getting to be a real sailor, she's handy as can be on the boat. We've got the races, and you've got to keep your boat up in between, and — well — there's all sorts of things." He paused a moment, looking at his father. "It looks like we can't make it this year. Next summer we'll come and see you."

"That's what you said last Christmas."

The girl looked faintly uncomfortable. The shape of their jawbones became more important in the arrangement of their faces.

The girl took up. "I don't see how we can do it, Dad. We've made engagements, all sorts of things. We can't change everything now." She leaned forward, speaking earnestly. "We're in the running for the Junior Cup; you wouldn't want to make us miss that."

The man worked his finger inside his collar, then he took a long drag on his cigarette, and watched the smoke as he blew it out. It was in him to lose his tongue or to plead, and he must do neither.

"All this — getting booked up the way you are — when you knew I was counting on you — did your mother — "

The boy cut in. "Mom's all right." It was definite, protective. "Mom says it's up to us to figure about seeing you."

"Yeah." He nodded. "Now listen — " He hesitated. He disliked the line he was going to take, but he had to take it. "Listen. I was all through the war. All that time, in the Pacific and all, I was counting on the time when I'd see you again. My big aim was to have you with me. I've planned my summer vacation just around that. Now don't you think that when a man gets out of the Army" (he kept himself from touching the Purple Heart) "he ought to expect that his children will want to come and visit him?"

He sounded corny and obvious to himself, but perhaps because of those very qualities, this time he reached them. There were several seconds of silence before the boy said,

"I guess that's right, Dad. Gee, I'm sorry. But we can't do it this year, don't you see? Let's say next summer."

The girl echoed, "Next summer."

He smoked, stared at his cigarette, hung back from a decision. Then his lips set firmly and he nodded to himself.

"Well I guess I'm just going to have to be tough. You've said 'next summer' before; I can't put any faith in that. So I'm just going to take you with me. I have the right, you know."

They looked at him, thunderstruck.

The girl said, "Oh no! You can't do that!" There was a wail in her voice.

The boy put his hand on his sister's. He spoke as if the man he was to be had entered into him. "You'll be awfully sorry if you do that, Dad. You'll just ruin the end of the summer for us, and you won't have any fun out of it."

The tone, the words, the firmness alarmed him. He studied them. The brightness was gone. In their faces under the shining hair he read stubbornness, appeal, and the beginning of hostility.

He got up abruptly, took a few paces away from them and back, then sat down again. He had lost them, lost them. He stared at nothing, trying to think. Two sullen children shanghaied to his cottage, angry among strangers, closed against his plans and arrangements, determined against him. He balanced that against their firm entrenchment here, the boat races and all the fixtures, which would continue summer after summer ever more enveloping, the continuity and custom which would make it always the wrong time for visiting their father. He wrestled with miserable alternatives. Finally he sighed deeply and his shoulders dropped.

"Okay. We'll let it go."

At once the light came back to their faces.

"Gee, that's swell, Dad."

"Oh, thanks a lot."

Their relief and bright looks were at once pleasure and pain. To salvage a shred of hope, without real conviction he said, "Then you'll come next summer? That's a promise?"

Next summer was in the unseeable future. "Sure, you bet."

"Sure thing."

He said, "All right." He wished their mother would come and get them. He had nothing more to say to them. "Let's get a coke." Anything to kill time.

She turned up about ten minutes later, blond, well-kept, smiling.

"Hello. Have a nice time?"

The boy said, "Yeah. We've had a swell time."

Joan added, "We're going to visit Dad next summer."

Their mother glanced briefly at the man and then at them. "That sounds very nice." She knew all right, she knew.

He exchanged politenesses with her, making himself as smiling as she was. The boy shook hands with him warmly, the girl put her face up to be kissed. The three went away, the smiling woman with the two clear-faced, tranquil children, both turned toward her. He stood rigid until they were out of sight.

To Walk in the City Streets

THE TAXI DRIVER, THE BELLHOP, THE DESK clerk identified them on sight as hillbilly runaways, as though they had personal knowledge of them. The driver saw them first, of course, at the depot; the man trying not to look uncertain, the girl's bewilderment only thinly covered. The man was very young, yet a man; he was tall, well-shouldered, obviously strong, and still a trifle too lanky for his strength. The girl was of good height, too, and well made, a strong girl, but her youngness was more pronounced, still in another category than his.

They were dressed in their Sunday best; the clothes themselves proclaimed it — her not-quite-fitting, not-quite-capturing-the-style, homemade dress and her naïve hat with too much on it; and his suit, little worn and also not quite fitting. It was visible in the way they wore them, not, in her case, the dress, which she wore with grace and enjoyment, but that hat, somehow uncertain of her head, as if hats were strange there. He made his suit appear stiff, the buttoned shirt collar and the necktie plainly oppressed him, and his small felt looked hard on his head. He had set the felt on square before they left the train, and from time to time his hand moved to it, making sure of its security. Each time, unconsciously, his hand moved it a trifle to the right, gradually approaching the slant at which he wore his broad and familiar straw hat, had worn it only the day before, getting in his father's hay.

Their baggage alone would have been enough to describe and place them. There was a worn, cardboard valise, and another, new one, and a big, antique Gladstone bag, the dry, rubbed leather of which had broken through at two of the bending corners. The driver swung the grips into the front of the cab, opened the rear door and smiled at them, although he knew they might be too ignorant to tip.

The two sat stiffly. After they had gone a few blocks, she said, "My, but it's big and noisy."

She was thinking of more than she said, so that her tone clearly showed that this comment was favorable. The bigness, the noisiness, could hide them. They could turn back his father, whose menace had stayed just behind them all the way out of the hills, through the county seat, apace with the clicking race of the train, and even across the state line. She had thought about it on the train, even in the forgetfulness of sitting beside him in the curious, polite privacy of a day coach, her shoulder touching his, their fingers intertwined. They had not left Charlesburg behind really, she thought, and where Charlesburg was, there that iron, willful tyrant's power also reached out. What now she saw through the taxi window was too big, too strong, for Charlesburg. She felt safety, and when his hand found hers, she knew from his touch that he did too.

The taxi stopped before the hotel they had named because Mrs. Nottingham, the minister's wife, once had stayed there. That it had no doorman did not signify to them. When the girl saw their grips on the sidewalk, here where there was not the crowding or the grime of a station platform, on the neat, exact cement, confronting the big glass doors, for the first time she realized how shabby they were, and she had a moment of doubt that made her mentally review her clothing, the dress copied from a picture, and look quickly at the young man. She found him smart, stiff, correct, and she was satisfied as to her own raiment.

He paid the driver carefully, out of a change purse. They had three days before he must report for induction, and their small funds had to be made to cover those three days and all the travel at each end. Three days would create a *fait accompli;* three days would create something that could not be undone, that not even his father could eliminate or undo. He paid the driver, and then, having twice traveled a little distance into the world with his father and thus learned something of what was correct, he selected a dime and handed it over. The driver said "Thanks," without sneering, liking the couple, liking their innocence and reading correctly the careful handling of that worn purse.

They did not find the lobby shabby — quite the reverse. In his two previous journeys he had seen none better, and she knew only the River House at Sudden Bend, the county seat, not to stay in, but to sit in one of the lobby rockers briefly, shyly, after the special extravagance of a lunch in its restaurant. In this lobby were some amazingly comfortable-looking leather armchairs, a number of wicker chairs and a table on which was a pot with a green shrub in it. There were half a dozen tall ash trays, and no spittoons. At the far end was the desk, electric-lighted, and on either side of it a stiff, thronelike chair with embossed leather on the back and many small brass-headed nails. In one of these chairs the bellhop reposed, inert, estivating. To one side was the elevator, its doors open, and beyond that, at the corner, a wooden staircase.

There was a door in the wall to the right, over which a lighted sign said OLDE COLONIAL COFFEE SHOPPE. Beside the door a placard on an easel announced a roast-beef special and stated the meal hours. In the opposite wall was another door, open, which had above it the words YE OAK TAVERNE — COCKTAIL LOUNGE. As they moved forward through the lobby, which was long enough to make its crossing an appreciable time with an increase of self-consciousness, the girl glanced sideways, to see all she could beyond that door without being caught gawking. In the lounge there was a blue semidarkness punctuated by spots of soft light, and at the far end the rainbow of a juke box, not then playing.

The desk clerk and the bellhop, neither of whom was young, identified them as the driver had. If clothes and possessions had not betrayed them, it was in their faces, more exposed now than in the station, where they had felt inconspicuous among the many people, the country look, hesitation, uncertainty and the underlying excitement which they believed they were concealing. The bellhop expressed his judgment by not moving to take their bags.

They stopped at the desk, the young man almost touching it, the girl half a step behind him, still holding the new valise. "We'd like a room for three days," he said, his voice level despite the tremendousness of his words.

The clerk pushed the card and pen toward him. He, having foreseen this, having thought about it and mentally rehearsed it a dozen times on the train, took the pen calmly, and, as though he were not thereby changing the world wrote "Mr. and Mrs. Jonas Hathaway." He hesitated no more than a moment before adding "Charlesburg," and omitted from his home address only the R.F.D. route. The girl watched this procedure with quiet admiration while at the same time her mind embraced the portentous written statement, "Mr. and Mrs." Like that, clear and deep blue on the white card, visible, permanent, conclusive.

The clerk said, "You and Mrs. Hathaway already married or you fixin' to get married?"

The young man looked up with an expression of pure, stony anger that was a complete answer in itself. In that anger, in the sudden set of his jaw, she saw his father, and yet something different from that terrible man's rage, for this, which he had never shown in her presence before, was generous, with concern for her name and for keeping this precious occasion unsmirched, and strong as it was, it was controlled. As she watched him, and the clerk resisted an instinct to step back out of danger, he checked himself, and said mildly, "We're married." He started to draw the certificate from his breast pocket. His father would have been incapable of stopping himself like that.

Every minute, it seemed, she learned more of him, and each new thing deepened her love. She had thought she knew him thoroughly, since childhood — which she conceived of as long left behind her — yet in the running away, in the wedding, in the traveling, she never ceased learning him anew.

The clerk said, "That's all right, sir. No offense, but we have to be careful, especially with strangers from out of the state. What kind of a room do you want?"

"What do they cost?"

"Without bath, from three-fifty up." Then, in revenge

for the moment of fear before the bright blaze of this country boy's eyes, he said, "But I guess you'll want the bridal suite. That's only twelve-fifty."

The young man stood motionless, slowly blushing, turned callow and helpless. Twelve-fifty was flatly impossible, but he was the husband, the bridegroom, and this was their day, so he stood wrestling, knowing it impossible and feeling ashamed.

The girl said, "We don't want no suite, Jo. We just want a nice room."

Rescued, he relaxed, and the redness ebbed from his face. "That's right. A nice room with bath."

She touched his elbow. "Where we can look out and see the city."

The clerk smiled. He had had his moment and he was content. "You'll want a double bed, of course. Let's see." He turned and ran his eyes over the pigeonholes with their keys and scattering diagonals of letters and messages, in doing which he gave them a chance to shake off the impact of that casual reference to a bed. "There's a very nice room on the second floor, overlooking the street. It's four-fifty."

Jonas said, "That will do fine."

The clerk said "Front, boy!" briskly and the bellhop moved forward in torpor. The clerk handed out a key. "Two-oh-five."

The man took the baggage and led them to the elevator, gloomily anticipating no tip, or a dime, his face aloof and withdrawn. For the girl, the elevator was as new as taxis with clicking meters running up white numbers on a black ground, or the streets in spate of traffic, or the sight of a blue-dark cocktail lounge. She went to it curiously, her hand firm but easy on her husband's arm, then tightening when the door closed and they were shut in a too-small, bright room. The elevator wheezed and moved, then it stopped, causing a sensation in her stomach, and the door sighed open.

It was a very long corridor, red-carpeted over all its length, with a multitude of doors, over a dozen on each side. At the far end was the relief of a window; otherwise, after the enclosed magic of the elevator, one could imagine that one was in unfathomable interior recesses lost forever from sunlight. The bellhop stopped at 205, unlocked the door, opened it and went in, seeing no need to waste deference upon these two. He put the old, worn Gladstone on the rack, set the two other pieces beside it, opened the closet door, turned on the light in the bathroom, then opened the window, letting in heat and the dull, constant voice of the city, set the key on the bureau, and said, "Anything else?"

Jonas stared at him a moment, said "Oh," and took out the purse, thinking hard. His father had said you tip, and although he did not like this man, in whom he felt a mean hostility, he would do what was becoming, but he would not himself be mean nor yet foolish. He took out a fifty-cent piece, amazing the man and bringing about a change in him.

"Thank you, sir. You want anything — ice water, or drinks, or anything — just pick up the phone." He pointed to it, then left.

The bed dominated the room. To sit on, apart from it, there were a moderately comfortable, comfortably worn armchair, and a straight chair, facing and tucked up against the table with the glass over its top on which the telephone rested. There was a bureau, also with glass covering its top, under which lay several rectangles of paper telling of laundry service and the hours and offerings of the coffee shop and cocktail lounge. Of free space, there seemed to be hardly as much altogether as that occupied by the bed. What they needed was a sofa, on which they could sit together in decency, or else two approximately equal chairs, placed side by side, but there was neither, so they stood, embarrassed. After some seconds, the girl's mouth formed in determination, and with decisive motions she put her handbag on the table beside the telephone; then she removed her hat and placed it on the closet shelf. In so doing she took possession; she was the woman, and for now this was where she kept house, where she put things in their places. Her husband became less rigid. He followed suit with his hat; then took off his coat, without which he felt much more at ease, and hung it on one of the wire hangers in the closet.

These actions brought both of them close to the bathroom door, where the light attracted their eyes. The girl gasped. Jonas almost did the same. Traveling with his father, he had never been in a room with a bath, and the shabby lavatories he had known had not at all prepared him for this gleaming chamber, all tiled, the lower portion light green, with the huge shining tub, the mirror, the glistening, semi-transparent shower curtain and the other fixtures. That there was a faint, brown stain under the hot-water tap in the washstand was insignificant, nor did they notice that there was a tear in the shower curtain, but the girl saw, with a certain sense of relief, that the window sill was grimy and should be wiped down. Like the bed, the bathroom proclaimed itself, and having it opening directly into their room seemed an indecency. They drew back and the girl closed the door firmly.

She moved to the window, drawn by the sounds of the

city, feeling security in every evidence of its vastness. She looked down at the street, the twin rivers of cars and trucks, the people on the hard sidewalk. The sun was not yet down, but it was low, shining the length of the harshly straight roadway from the west to throw spidery, stretched-out caricature shadows of the walkers, which she watched with fascination. Down the block on the right was a moving-picture theater, and she reflected immediately that by going to it after, in a short time, they had eaten supper, they would solve what had begun to loom in her mind as a difficult problem of a gap in time — a period after eating when to sit in this bed-filled room together or to sit in the lobby publicly would be equally disagreeable in different ways.

She noticed a sudden appearance of colored light out of the corner of her eye, and looked to the left, to see an elaborated sign, its neon just turned on, which announced in curiously shaped letters, THE CANTON PAGODA, while simpler characters, red and blue across the windows, stated, CHINESE AND AMERICAN FOOD, and CHOP SUEY. She had heard tell of Chinese restaurants, and it seemed to her that their voyage would have extended to farther places, the experiences would have been vastly deeper, her knowledge of the outside, great world enhanced, if Jonas would take her to eat there. Then she thought that being foreign, it would probably be too expensive for them, but there might be some moderately priced dish. There was a rectangle of white on the corner of one window, which, she thought, was probably a bill of fare, so that it would be possible to learn the prices without going inside. Jonas, she knew, would as lief have his hand cut off as to walk into such a place, ask about cost, and then walk out without buying anything.

Up to then, she had been taken up with the business of

running away, the fear of pursuit and the overwhelming fact of her wedding day. She had thought of the city in terms of the protection that it might offer, food and shelter. Now the excitement of being in such a place, the explorations to be performed, the things to be seen, heard, tasted, crowded into consciousness. She decided that they should go down right away and walk a little in that crowded street; then that she would like to go into the cocktail lounge and find out what one was like, and try one of those complex, wonderfully flavored drinks that she had heard of. She knew only the taste of elderberry and dandelion wines, mildly hard cider, and the vileness of one experimental sip of crude whiskey. She would taste a cocktail, and before that they would have found out whether the Chinese place was within their range, or whether they had better try the Olde Colonial Coffee Shoppe — but that special was no bargain — or perhaps somewhere else. In a city like this there would be many eating places, of many kinds and prices.

She was about to turn to her husband when she saw the dusty, gray four-door sedan draw up in front of the hotel door. She drew in a sharp breath and froze, watching the big man get out, moving slowly, as was his way. So much heavier as he was, between his shoulders and Jonas' there was a strong resemblance.

She faced toward her husband and said, "Your pa's here. He just got out of his car."

The young man stared at her. "They won't let him up without we say so." He said it as if he wished to make it true, rather than really believed that anyone could turn his father back.

The girl reached decision suddenly and completely. "You better go down and tackle him."

He looked at her blankly. "No. I — " His voice trailed off.

"Jonas Hathaway, you go down and tackle him." She spoke firmly. "You got to sooner or later, and it might as well be now. And I ain't goin' to camp in this room afraid to step outside. So you'd best settle it now." Then, in a gentler voice, "You can do it, Jo."

The young man nodded slowly. "I guess I can." He straightened, and his mouth set again, firm. Anyone would have been conscious of the hard jaw line. He put on his coat and opened the door; then he looked back, smiled wryly, and said, "Here goes. You can put up a prayer for me." He went out, shutting the door firmly.

She sat down in the armchair. His expression, his voice, his way of moving, during the last few seconds before he left, were clear in her mind. The telephone rang. She let it ring. He had gone down without being summoned, and nothing should be done that would allow any doubt of that. Her mind remained suspended until the ringing stopped; then, with the silence, she was thinking again. This was probably the best thing that could have happened, head on, right at the start. It was going to be all right; there was no question about that. Folding her hands in her lap, she offered up a prayer, for prayer was always suitable, but she was in no doubt. It was not only that the city had weakened, attenuated, diluted Mr. Hathaway, but that she knew Jonas' capabilities now almost better than he did. She was not in the least afraid. She sat calmly, waiting for her husband to return and take her out to walk in the city streets.

Prelude to
Reunion

THE ROOM WAS FURNISHED WITH WHAT THE
college issued: a desk, placed dead center under the white
overhead light, a table, three wooden chairs, a bed, a
bureau, an empty fireplace the brick floor of which was
free of ashes or cigarette butts. One shelf of the bookcase
was almost filled with textbooks, a one-volume edition of
Shakespeare, and a Bible. Two notebooks and a dictionary
stood between the book ends on the desk. The table carried
a glass, a cup and saucer, a plate, and a small electric stove
with a saucepan on it. A calendar and two pine cones had
been arranged with an effort at decoration on the mantel-
piece. There was a framed photograph of a middle-aged
woman on the bureau, and two neckties hung from a corner
of the mirror. Under the adequate, neutral light, the room
looked as if its occupant had moved in that afternoon and
would leave tomorrow.

The boy paced slowly, methodically, between the fireplace and the bookcase. Going toward the fireplace, he

passed on the door side of the desk, returning, he took the window side. There was a difference; nearer the window he caught a stronger smell of the night, the new, disturbing mildness of spring was more emphatic, and he could hear voices below on the campus more clearly. He was tall, thin, fair-haired, with too much Adam's apple and too long a nose. He was not thinking, he was stringing out the time before he should decide to take a walk, just as the perfect tidying away of his papers strung it out.

He did not contemplate the foreknown procedure. He would put on necktie and coat, and go downstairs. As he stepped outside, he would feel a faint anticipation, a nameless, automatic stirring of hope, which he would quickly discount by a defensive reflex, a moment of pain never admitted. Then he would stroll. If he met fellows who sat in his classes, he would walk a little faster until he passed them, but sometimes even so they would remember him and nod, or say "Hello," or even "Hello, Matterson." He would say "Hello," and go on by, letting them continue their appointed ways. His own pace, too, would be a declaration that he was going somewhere.

By one route or another he would come to the Women's School. Here his walk would be a swinging, unhesitating stride. He would not turn his head, he would just go on through, but his eyes would take in a wide range, the groups of girls and the pairs of girls and fellows. Last week, the first night of the warm weather, a man who sat next him in Biochemistry, passed him with a girl. He said, "Hi, Matterson, sparking?" He'd said, "Hello, Newman, just scouting," and Newman and the girl had laughed.

They were all just kids, really: as old as he, but nothing had taught them seriousness. His brain could run rings around them. He wasn't interested in their eternal play.

Beyond the School, he would come out into the town. There he would buy a paper. Having the paper under his arm threw a bridge of occupation over the return to his room.

He walked up and down, preparing his legs for tiredness, not thinking what he was going to do next.

A firm knock at his door brought him up sharp. He moved to open it, checked himself, stood back and called, "Come in!"

The visitor, who entered rather self-consciously, was a well-dressed boy of medium height, neither fair nor dark, with a scrubbed, healthy face.

"Matterson?" he said. "I'm Bill Farraday. May I come in?"

"Hello. Sit down." His anger at himself for being so tense added to his stiffness.

"I live in this entry, 2B."

Matterson knew well enough, as he knew that Farraday had his letter in hockey, and was a candidate for class marshall. He nodded, watchful.

Farraday arranged himself with an effect of relaxation for which the chair was not well adapted. He looked around the room, said, "Nice — " then broke off. The thin boy understood, it was not a nice joint. Seeing that his visitor was ill at ease, he felt a shade more comfortable.

"Looks like spring had really come, doesn't it?" Farraday said. He became more assured at the sound of his own voice. "Here the winter's over, and this is the first time I've been up here." Matterson listened, guarded, protecting himself. "This college is so damn big, you can't hope to know everyone, but I'd promised myself to meet all the men in this entry. You know how it is, you get tied up in so many things, and the first thing you know the ice has melted, and the ball team's coming out of the cage."

Matterson said, "Yeah." He could imagine himself knowing.

"Where do you come from? You're not from around here, are you?"

"Vermont."

"Well. Why did you pick to come here?"

"I'm going into analytical chemistry, and I wanted to be under MacPherson."

"Oh. Oh, yeah, sure." Farraday paused again, then took off as if from a cue. "You had a scholarship?"

"Not to start with; the first two years I worked my way. Then I got the Bernstein." He was proud of that, it was the best there was in science for undergraduates. "Now I'm hoping for the Marlin Fellowship, if I can get my *magna cum* all right."

Farraday looked vaguely uncomfortable. The look passed. "Good for you. I admire a guy like you, and I'm glad I came up." Again his flow of talk became smooth. His voice had a flattering frankness. "Yeah; when I get out of here I'll go to Wall Street, and I guess that twenty years from now I'll be just another bond salesman living the old country-club life, and I'll be bragging on how I know you. I've had it easy and you've had it tough."

The Vermonter felt an unfamiliar warmth run through him. "It's been tough sometimes," he said. He hesitated, then added with an effort, "I saw you shoot that long goal against Colmouth."

"Oh, that was just luck." Farraday was visibly pleased. He pulled out a pack of cigarettes. "Smoke?"

"No, thanks."

"Oh. Do you mind — "

"Go ahead."

"Come down to my rooms sometime, won't you? Sling the bull, you know. I generally have a little beer on hand — or ginger ale."

"I like beer." He considered explaining that he didn't smoke on account of the expense, then decided not to.

Farraday brightened. "That's fine. I mean it, drop in."

"Thanks." He wanted to say more, but didn't know how.

"Say, a man like you, working your way along, and then getting fellowships and things — I'd like your slant on this endowment business."

Matterson had read the ballyhoo with a mounting sense of discomfort. The university was driving for extra endowment, and the Class Committee had voted a graduation gift of fifteen thousand dollars, which made a little over twenty dollars per member. It was getting a big play from the publicity bureau in going after the graduates.

"Well," he said, "I guess it's a good idea."

"Yeah, I think so, too. Our tuition fees don't cover the cost of our education — when you average it up, the men on scholarships and things, the University gives us each nearly a thousand dollars." Farraday caught himself up. "Of course," he said hastily, "that's what you expect the old place to do, help men like you who really have the brains. It's part of a University's proper function." He looked around. "Got an ashtray?"

"Chuck it in the fireplace."

He did so, then pulled out the pack again. "I guess I'm smoking a lot right now. What with the finals coming on, and all the boning to do, and one thing and another, I get kind of nervous." He lit up. "This endowment business on top of the rest, has me about daffy. You see, I'm in charge of this entry, and we're short on our quota. I dunno how it is, some of the fellows don't seem to appreciate what the old school does for them. I guess I'm a rotten collector; it kind of burns me up to get after a man if he isn't willing." He gave a short, unreal laugh. "Yeah, I hate doing it. I've upped my share to fifty bucks, though God knows I guess it means the sheriff will be after me, what with the old unpaid bills and all." He made the last statement with a smile, as one man speaking to another of a common problem.

Matterson just watched him, saying nothing. He looked dull, withdrawn.

"I've got you down for five bucks," Farraday said. "Of course, it's up to you. You know what you can afford, spreading it over the next three months."

Matterson continued staring at him. Out of a swirl inside himself he said quietly, without a shade of defiance in his tone, "You can put me down for ten."

"Why say, that's great. Say, that's the real spirit, Matterson. Wait till I tell some of the other men that, the ones who've been holding out." He pulled at his cigarette, held it a moment, threw it in the fireplace. "Yeah, that's great. Well, look, I've got to get after some of the others now." He rose. "Don't forget to drop in on me sometime."

Matterson said, "Sure. Thanks."

Farraday answered heartily. "Thanks to you. Well, so long. Be seeing you."

"So long."

He sat and stared at the long awaited, casual disorder of the two cigarette stubs in the fireplace, then he stood with his hands in his pockets. Ten dollars was catastrophic. Double what the rich boy thought him good for — pride stiffened in him, covering the pain of a warm moment betrayed. More slowly than usual, he tied his necktie, put on his coat, and went out.

The
Resting Place

THE POSSIBILITY THAT DR. HILLEBRAND WAS
developing kleptomania caused a good deal of pleasure
among his younger colleagues — that is, the entire personnel of the Department of Anthropology, including its
director, Walter Klibben. It was not that anybody really
disliked the old boy. That would have been hard to do, for
he was co-operative and gentle, and his humor was mild;
he was perhaps the greatest living authority on Southwestern
archaeology, and broadly learned in the general science of
anthropology; and he was a man who delighted in the success of others.

Dr. Hillebrand was the last surviving member of a group
of men who had made the Department of Anthropology
famous in the earlier part of the twentieth century. His
ideas were old-fashioned; to Walter Klibben, who at forty
was very much the young comer, and to the men he had
gathered about him, Dr. Hillebrand's presence, clothed with
authority, was as incongruous as that of a small, mild bron-
tosaurus would be in a modern farmyard.

On the other hand, no one living had a finer archaeological technique. Added to this was a curious intuition,
which caused him to dig in unexpected places and come up
with striking finds — the kind of thing that delights donors
and trustees, such as the largest unbroken Mesa Verde black-
on-white jar known up to that time, the famous Biltabito
Cache of turquoise and shell objects, discovered two years
before and not yet on exhibition, and, only the previous
year, the mural decorations at Painted Mask Ruin. The
mural, of which as yet only a small part had been uncovered,
compared favorably with the murals found at Awatovi and
Kawaika-a by the Peabody Museum, but was several centuries older. Moreover, in the part already exposed there
was an identifiable katchina mask, unique and conclusive
evidence that the katchina cult dated back to long before
the white man came. This meant, Dr. Klibben foresaw
gloomily, that once again all available funds for publication
would be tied up by the old coot's material.

The trustees loved him. Several years ago, he had reached
the age of retirement and they had waived the usual limi-
tation in his case. He was curator of the museum, a position
only slightly less important than that of director, and he
occupied the Kleinman Chair in American Archaeology.
This was an endowed position paying several thousand a
year more than Klibben's own professorship.

Dr. Hillebrand's occupancy of these positions, on top of
his near monopoly of publication money, was the rub. He
blocked everything. If only the old relic would become
emeritus, the younger men could move up. Klibben had it
all worked out. There would be the Kleinman Chair for
himself, and McDonnell could accede to his professorship.
He would leave Steinberg an associate, but make him cura-

tor. Thus, Steinberg and McDonnell would have it in mind that the curatorship always might be transferred to Mc-Donnell as the man with senior status, which would keep them both on their toes. At least one assistant professor could, in due course, be made an associate, and young George Franklin, Klibben's own prized student, could be promoted from instructor to assistant. It all fitted together and reinforced his own position. Then, given free access to funds for monographs and papers . . .

But Dr. Hillebrand showed no signs of retiring. It was not that he needed the money from his two positions; he was a bachelor and something of an ascetic, and much of his salary he put into his own expeditions. He loved to teach, he said — and his students liked him. He loved his museum; in fact, he was daffy about it, pottering around in it until late at night. Well, let him retire, and he could still teach a course or two if he wanted; he could still potter, but Klibben could run his Department as he wished, as it ought to be run.

Since there seemed no hope that the old man would give out physically in the near future, Klibben had begun looking for symptoms of mental failure. There was, for instance, the illogical way in which Dr. Hillebrand often decided just where to run a trench or dig a posthole. As Steinberg once remarked, it was as if he were guided by a ouija board. Unfortunately, this eccentricity produced splendid results.

Then, sometimes Hillebrand would say to his students, "Now, let us imagine — " and proceed to indulge in surprising reconstructions of the daily life and religion of the ancient cliff dwellers, going far beyond the available evidence. The director had put Franklin onto that, because the young man had worked on Hopi and Zuñi ceremonial.

Franklin reported that the old boy always made it clear that these reconstructions were not science, and, further, Franklin said that they were remarkably shrewd and had given him some helpful new insights into aspects of the modern Indians' religion.

The possibility of kleptomania was something else again. The evidence — insufficient so far — concerned the rich Biltabito Cache, which Dr. Hillebrand himself was enumerating, cataloguing, and describing, mostly evenings, when the museum was closed. He was the only one who knew exactly how many objects had been in the find, but it did look as if some of it might now be missing. There was also what the night watchman thought he had seen. And then there was that one turquoise bead — but no proof it had come from that source, of course — that McDonnell had found on the floor near the cast of the Quiriguá stela, just inside the entrance to the museum.

The thefts — if there had been any — had taken place in April and early May, when everyone was thinking of the end of the college year and the summer's field trips. A short time later, and quite by accident, Klibben learned from an associate professor of ornithology that old Hillebrand had obtained from him a number of feathers, which he said he wanted for repairing his collection of katchina dolls. Among them were parrot and macaw feathers, and the fluffy feathers from the breast of an eagle.

Klibben's field was not the American Southwest, but any American anthropologist would have been able to draw an obvious conclusion: turquoise, shell, and feathers of those sorts were components of ritual offerings among the modern Hopis and Zuñis, and possibly their ancestors, among whose remains Dr. Hillebrand had carried on his lifework. Dr.

Klibben began to suspect — or hope — that the old man was succumbing to a mental weakness far more serious than would be evidenced by the mere stealing of a few bits of turquoise and shell.

The director made tactful inquiries at the genetics field laboratory to see if the old man had been seeking corn pollen, another component of the ritual offerings, and found that there the question of the evolution of *Zea maiz* in the Southwest was related to the larger and much vexed question of the origin and domestication of that important New World plant, so interesting to archaeologists, botanists, and geneticists. Dr. Hillebrand had been collecting specimens of ancient corn from archaeological sites for a long time — ears, cobs, and grains extending over two millenniums or more, and other parts of the plant, including some fragments of tassels. It was, Klibben thought, the kind of niggling little detail you would expect to find Hillebrand spending good time on. Dr. Hillebrand had been turning his specimens over to the plant and heredity boys, who were delighted to have them. They, in turn, had followed this up by obtaining — for comparison — seed of modern Pueblo Indian, Navajo, and Hopi corn, and planting it. It was natural enough, then, that from to time Dr. Hillebrand should take specimens of seed and pollen home to study on his own. It might be clear as day to Klibben that the old boy had gone gaga to the point of making ritual offerings to the gods of the cliff dwellings; he still had nothing that would convince a strongly pro-Hillebrand board of trustees.

Even so, the situation was hopeful. Klibben suggested to the night watchman that, out of concern for Professor Hillebrand's health, he keep a special eye on the Professor's afterhours activities in the museum. Come June, he would arrange for Franklin — with his Southwestern interests, Franklin was the logical choice — to go along on Hillebrand's expedition and see what he could see.

Franklin took the assignment willingly, by no means unaware of the possible advantages to himself should the old man be retired. The archaeologist accepted this addition to his staff with equanimity. He remarked that Franklin's knowledge of Pueblo daily life would be helpful in interpreting what might be uncovered, while a better grounding in Southwestern prehistory would add depth to the young man's ethnographic perceptions. Right after commencement, they set out for the Navajo country of Arizona, accompanied by two undergraduate and four graduate students.

At Farmington, in New Mexico, they picked up the university's truck and station wagon and Hillebrand's own field car, a Model A Ford as archaic as its owner. In view of the man's income, Franklin thought, his hanging on to the thing was one more oddity, an item that could be added to many others to help prove Klibben's case. At Farmington, too, they took on a cook and general helper. Dr. Hillebrand's work was generously financed, quite apart from what went into it from his own earnings.

The party bounced over the horrifying road past the Four Corners and around the north end of Beautiful Mountain, into the Chinlee Valley, then southward and westward until, after having taken a day and a half to drive about two hundred miles, they reached the cliffs against which stood Painted Mask Ruin. The principal aim of the current summer's work was to excavate the decorated kiva in detail, test another kiva, and make further, standard excavations in the ruin as a whole.

By the end of a week, the work was going nicely. Dr. Hillebrand put Franklin, as the senior scientist under him, in charge of the work in the painted kiva. Franklin knew perfectly well that he was deficient in the required techniques; he would, in fact, be dependent upon his first assistant, Philip Fleming, who was just short of his Ph.D. Fleming had worked in that kiva the previous season, had spent three earlier seasons with Dr. Hillebrand, and was regarded by him as the most promising of the many who had worked under him. There was real affection between the two men.

Two of the other graduate students were well qualified to run a simple dig for themselves. One was put in charge of the untouched second kiva, the other of a trench cutting into the general mass of the ruin from the north. Franklin felt uncomfortably supernumerary, but he recognized that that was an advantage in pursuing his main purpose of keeping a close watch on the expedition's director.

After supper on the evening of the eighth day, Dr. Hillebrand announced rather shyly that he would be gone for about four days, "to follow an old custom you all know about." The younger men smiled. Franklin kept a blank face to cover his quickened interest.

This was a famous, or notorious, eccentricity of the old man's, and one in which Drs. Klibben, McDonnell, and the rest put great hope. Every year, early in the season, Dr. Hillebrand went alone to a ruin he had excavated early in his career. There was some uncertainty as to just where the ruin was; it was believed to be one known to the Navajos as Tsekaiye Kin. No one knew what he did there. He said he found the surroundings and the solitude invaluable for thinking out the task in hand. It was usually not long after his return from it that he would announce his decision to dig in such-and-such a spot, and proceed to uncover the painted kiva, or the Kettle Cave fetishes, or the Kin Hatsosi blanket, or some other notable find.

If Franklin could slip away in the station wagon and follow the old man, he might get just the information he wanted. So far, Dr. Hillebrand's activities on the expedition had evidenced nothing but his great competence. If the old man ever performed mad antique rites with stolen specimens, it would be at his secret place of meditation. Perhaps he got up and danced to the ancient gods. One might be able to sneak a photo . . .

Dr. Hillebrand said, "I shan't be gone long. Meantime, of course, Dr. Franklin will be in charge." He turned directly to his junior. "George, there are several things on which you must keep a close watch. If you will look at these diagrams — and you, too, Phil . . ."

Franklin and Fleming sat down beside him. Dr. Hillebrand expounded. Whether the ancient devil had done it intentionally or not, Franklin saw that he was neatly hooked. In the face of the delicacy and the probable outcome of the next few days' work, he could not possibly make an excuse for absenting himself when the head of the expedition was also absent.

Dr. Hillebrand took off early the next morning in his throbbing Model A. He carried with him a Spartan minimum of food and bedding. It was good to be alone once more in the long-loved reaches of the Navajo country. The car drove well. He still used it because, short of a jeep, nothing newer had the clearance to take him where he wanted to go.

He drove slowly, for he was at the age when knowledge

and skill must replace strength, and getting stuck would be serious. When he was fifty, he reflected, he would have reached T'iiz Hatsosi Canyon from this year's camp in under four hours; when he was thirty, if it had been possible then to travel this country in a car, he would have made even greater speed, and as like as not ended by getting lost. He reached the open farming area outside the place where T'iiz Hatsosi sliced into the great mesa to the south. There were nearly twice as many hogans to be seen as when he had first come here; several of them were square and equipped with windows, and by some of them cars were parked. Everything was changing, but these were good people still, although not as genial and hospitable as their grandparents had been when he first packed in.

He entered the narrow mouth of T'iiz Hatsosi Canyon in the late afternoon, and by the exercise of consummate skill drove some four miles up it. At that point, it was somewhat wider than elsewhere, slightly under two hundred feet across at the bottom. The heavy grazing that had so damaged all the Navajos' land had had some effect here. There was less grass than there used to be — but then, he reflected, he had no horses to pasture — and the bed of the wash was more deeply eroded, and here and there sharp gullies led into it from the sides.

Still, the cottonwoods grew between the occasional stream and the high, warmly golden-bluff cliffs. Except at noon, there was shade, and the quality of privacy, almost of secrecy, remained. In the west wall was the wide strip of white rock from which the little ruin took its name, Tsekaiye Kin, leading the eye to the long ledge above which the cliff arched like a scallop shell, and upon which stood the ancient habitations. The lip of the ledge was about twenty feet above the level of the canyon, and approachable by a talus slope that was not too hard to negotiate. Some small evergreens grew at the corners of the ledge. From the ground, the settlement did not seem as if it had been empty for centuries, but rather as if its occupants at the moment happened not to be visible. The small black rectangles of doorways and three tiny squares of windows made him feel, as they had done over forty years ago, as if the little settlement were watching him.

South of the far end of the ledge, and at the level of the canyon floor, was the spring. Water seeped richly through a crack in the rock a few feet above the ground and flowed down over rock to form a pool at the base. The wet golden-brown stone glistened; small water growths clung to the crevices. In the pool itself, there was cress, and around it moss and grass rich enough to make a few feet of turf.

Here Dr. Hillebrand deposited his bedroll and his food. He estimated that he had better than two hours of daylight left. He cut himself a supply of firewood. Then he took a package out of his coffeepot. The package was wrapped in an old piece of buckskin. With this in hand, he climbed up the slope to the ruin.

The sense of peace had begun once he was out of sight of the camp at Painted Mask Ruin. It had grown when he entered T'iiz Hatsosi Canyon; it had become stronger when he stepped out of the car and glimpsed through the cotton-woods his little village, with its fourteen rooms. By the spring, it had become stronger yet, and mixed with a nostalgia of past times that was sweetly painful, like a memory of an old and good lost love. These feelings were set aside as he addressed himself to the task of climbing, which was not entirely simple; then they returned fourfold when he was in the ruin. Here he had worked alone, a green young man with a shiny new Doctor's degree, a boy-man not unlike young Fleming. Here he had discovered what it was like to step into a room that still had its roof intact, and see the marks of the smoke from the houschold fire, the loom ties still in place in the ceiling and floor, the broken cooking pot still in the corner.

He paid his respects to that chamber — Room 4-B; stood in the small, open, central area; then went to the roofless, irregular oval of the kiva. All by himself he had dug it out.

Could Dr. Franklin have been there, spying unseen, he would have been most happy. From under a stone that appeared firmly embedded in the clay flooring Dr. Hillebrand took an ancient, crude stone pipe fitted with a recent willow stem. He filled it with tobacco, performed curious motions as he lit it, and puffed smoke in the six directions. Then he climbed out of the kiva on the inner side and went behind the double row of habitations, to the darker area under the convex curve of the wall at the back of the cave, the floor of which was a mixture of earth and rubbish. Two smallish, rounded stones about three feet apart inconspicuously marked a place. Sitting by it on a convenient ledge of rock, he puffed at the pipe again; then he opened the buckskin package and proceeded to make an offering of ancient turquoise beads, white and red shell, black stone, feathers and down, and corn pollen.

Sitting back comfortably, he said, "Well, here I am again."

The answer did not come from the ground, in which the bones of the speaker reposed, but from a point in space, as if he were sitting opposite Dr. Hillebrand. "Welcome, old friend. Thank you for the gifts; their smell is pleasing to us all."

"I don't know whether I can bring you any more," the

archaeologist said. "I can buy new things, of course, but getting the old ones is becoming difficult. They are watching me."

"It is not necessary," the voice answered. "We are rich in the spirits of things such as these, and our grandchildren on earth still offer them to us. It has been rather for your benefit that I have had you bringing them, and I think that that training has served its purpose."

"You relieve me." Then, with a note of anxiety, "That doesn't mean that I have to stop visiting you?"

"Not at all. And, by the way, there is a very handsome jar with a quantity of beans of an early variety in it where you are digging now. It was left behind by accident when the people before the ones who built the painted kiva moved out. It belonged to a woman called Bluebird Tailfeather. Her small child ran off and was lost just as they were moving, and by the time she found him, the war chief was impatient. However, we can come back to that later. I can see that you have something on your mind."

"I'm lonely," Dr. Hillebrand said simply. "My real friends are all gone. There are a lot of people I get on nicely with, but no one left I love — that is, above the ground — and you are the only one below the ground I seem to be able to reach. I — I'd like to take your remains back with me, and then we could talk again."

"I would not like that."

"Then of course I won't."

"I was sure of that. Your country is strange to me, and traveling back and forth would be a lot of effort. What I saw that time I visited you was alien to me; it would be to you, too, I think. It won't be long, I believe, before I am relieved of attachment to my bones entirely, but if you moved them now, it would be annoying. You take that burial you carried home ten years ago — old Rabbit Stick. He says you treat him well and have given him the smell of ceremonial jewels whenever you could, but sometimes he arrives quite worn out from his journey."

"Rabbit Stick," Dr. Hillebrand mused. "I wondered if there were not someone there. He has never spoken to me."

"He couldn't. He was just an ordinary Reed Clan man. But he is grateful to you for the offerings, because they have given him the strength he needed. As you know, I can speak with you because I was the Sun's Forehead, and there was the good luck that you were thinking and feeling in the right way when you approached me. But tell me, don't the young men who learn from you keep you company?"

"Yes. There is one now who is like a son to me. But then they have learned, and they go away. The men in between, who have become chiefs, you might say, in my Department, have no use for me. They want to make me emeritus — that is, put me on a pension, take over my authority and my rewards, and set me where I could give advice and they could ignore it. They have new ways, and they despise mine. So now they are watching me. They have sent a young man out this time just to watch me. They call him a student of the ways of your grandchildren; he spent six weeks at Zuñi once, and when even he could see that the people didn't like him, he went and put in the rest of the summer at Oraibi."

"New Oraibi or Old Oraibi?" the Sun's Forehead asked.

"New Oraibi."

The chief snorted.

"So, having also read some books, he thinks he is an ethnographer, only he calls himself a cultural anthropologist.

And he is out here to try to find proof that my mind is failing." He smiled. "They'd certainly think so if they saw me sitting here talking to empty air."

The Sun's Forehead chuckled. "They certainly would. They wouldn't be able to hear me, you know." Then his voice became serious again. "That always happens, I think. It happened to me. They wanted to do things differently, when I had at last come to the point at which an Old Man talked to me. I reached it in old age — not young, as you did. They could not take my title, but they wanted to handle my duties for me, bring me enough food to live on, hear my advice and not listen to it. Struggling against them became wearying and distasteful, so finally I decided to go under. At the age I reached — about your age — it is easy to do."

"And now you say that you are about to be detached from your bones entirely? You are reaching the next stage?"

"Let us say that I begin to hope. Our life is beautiful, but for a hundred years or so now I have been longing for the next, and I begin to hope."

"How does it happen? Or is it wrong for me to know?"

"You may know. You are good, and you keep your secrets, as our wise men always did. You will see a man who has become young, handsome, and full of light. When we dance, he dances with great beauty; his singing is beautiful, and you feel as if it were creating life. Then one time when the katchinas themselves are dancing before us — not masks, you understand, the katchinas themselves — you can't find him among the watchers. Then you seem to recognize him, there among the sacred people, dancing like them. Then you think that the next time our grandchildren on the earth put on the masks and dance, that one, whom

you knew as a spirit striving to purify himself, who used
to tell you about his days on earth, will be there. With
his own eyes he will see our grandchildren and bless them."
The chief's voice trailed off, as though the longing for what
he was describing deprived him of words.

"To see the katchinas themselves dancing," Dr. Hillebrand mused. "Not the masks, but what the masks stand
for . . . That would keep me happy for centuries. But
then, I could not join your people. I was never initiated.
I'd be plain silly trying to dance with them. It's not for me."

"For over forty years I have been initiating you," the
Sun's Forehead said. "As for dancing — you will no longer
be in that old body. You will not be dancing with those
fragile, rheumatic bones. There is room for you in our
country. Why don't you come over? Just lie down in that
crevice back there and make up your mind."

"You know," Dr. Hillebrand said, "I think I will."

Both the Kleinman Professor of American Archaeology
and the spirit who once had been the Sun's Forehead for
the settlements in the neighborhood of T'iiz Hatsosi were
thoroughly unworldly. It had not occurred to either of
them that within six days after Dr. Hillebrand had left
camp Dr. George Franklin would organize a search for him,
and four days later his body would be found where he had
died of, apparently, heart failure. Above all, it had not
occurred to them that his body would be taken home and
buried with proper pomp and ceremony in the appropriate
cemetery. (But Philip Fleming, close to tears, resolutely
overlooked the scattering of turquoise and shell in the rubbish between the crevice and the kiva.)

Dr. Hillebrand found himself among people as alien to
him as they had been to the Sun's Forehead. They seemed

to be gaunt from the total lack of offerings, and the means by which they should purify and advance themselves to where they could leave this life for the next, which he believed to be the final one, were confused. He realized that his spirit was burdened with much dross, and that it would be a long time before he could gather the strength to attempt a journey to the country of his friend.

His portrait, in academic gown and hood, was painted posthumously and hung in the entrance of the museum, to one side of the stela from Quiriguá and facing the reproduction of the famous Painted Kiva mural. Dr. Klibben adroitly handled the promotions and emoluments that fell under his control. Philip Fleming won his Ph.D. with honor, and was promptly offered a splendid position at Harvard. Moved by he knew not what drive, and following one or two other actions he had performed to his own surprise, Fleming went to Dr. Hillebrand's grave, for a gesture of respect and thanks.

It had seemed to him inappropriate to bring any flowers. Instead, as he sat by the grave, with small motions of his hands he sprinkled over it some bits of turquoise and shell he had held out from a necklace he had unearthed, and followed them with a pinch of pollen given him by a Navajo. Suddenly his face registered utter astonishment; then careful listening.

The following season, Fleming returned to Painted Mask Ruin by agreement with Dr. Klibben, who was delighted to get his Department entirely out of Southwestern archaeology. There he ran a trench that led right into a magnificent polychrome pot containing a store of beans of high botanical interest.

Within a few years, he stopped visiting the grave, but he

was sentimentalist enough to make a pilgrimage all alone to Tsekaiye Kin at the beginning of each field season. It was jokingly said among his confreres that there he communed with the spirit of old Hillebrand. Certainly he seemed to have inherited that legendary figure's gift for making spectacular finds.

The Happy
Indian Laughter

THREE MEN SAT, EACH ON ONE OF THREE
wooden steps. The one on the top step was young. His
hair was cut short. He wore a fairly large, neat, light gray
Stetson, a blue Air Force officer's shirt, a blue silk scarf at
his throat, neatly pressed Levis, and cowboy boots. He was
waiting for something. He sat as quietly as the others, but
you could tell that he was waiting.

The two others were past middle age. Their large black
felt hats were battered. One had a beadwork hatband, the
other a hatband made of dimes. From under the hatbrims,
just behind their ears, their braided hair hung down,
wrapped in two colors of tape, crisscrossing. These two
were not waiting for anything, they were just relaxing.

When a big blue convertible with the top up came around
the corner at the end of the dusty street, all three looked up.
The car seemed to hesitate, then came toward them slowly.

The man on the middle step said, "Tourists." He looked

at the one below him, who was thin, and older than he. "Show your moccasins, brother; perhaps they'll pay to take your picture."

"Run tell your wife to weave a basket."

They both laughed. The young man's face had become blank.

The old man said, "Just one tourist — a woman, young. Perhaps we can be Apaches and frighten her."

The two laughed again — the pleasant, light laughter of Indians. The young man said, using a title of respect, "Grandfather, I know this woman. She was a friend when I was in the Air Force."

The old man said, "Good. Let her walk in peace."

The girl had put up the top of her convertible when she encountered the penetrating dust of the road that led from the sad little town of Arenosa to the Indian Agency. The road appalled her. The dirt was hard, cut by ruts, and washboarded, and, for all its hardness, produced fine, clayey dust in quantity. She came to a cattle guard, a strong barbed-wire fence, and a sign reading, "Department of the Interior — U.S. Indian Service — Gohlquain Apache Indian Reservation — No Trespassing." She stopped the car and studied the sign, half minded to turn back. Then, with a jerk, she started forward again. She had overcome too much opposition, in herself and from others, to turn back now.

The Agency was five miles inside the boundary, Ralph had written, and the high country of grass and trees not far beyond. She could see the high country ahead of her, blue and inscrutable. She'd find out soon enough what it was really like. She'd find out a lot, and above all the difference between a handsome — you could almost say beautiful — Air Force pilot with a bronze skin and an Apache cattleman. As she had pointed out to friends and relatives, he was a college man as well as a pilot, and he would be the same in any setting, with the same nice manners and the same humor. She wished now that she were sure of that.

The Agency was a village, strung out along a wide, straight section of the road. There were white wooden houses, some adobe ones, and a couple of dreary brick buildings. Ralph had written that he would be waiting for her in front of the Agency proper, which she could recognize by the sign over its door and the clock in the little tower on top. She came almost to a stop, looked about, then proceeded slowly.

She passed two women walking in the opposite direction, on her side of the road. Their hair hung, rich and black, over their shoulders. They wore calico blouses and full calico skirts. As she passed them, they did not glance but looked at her for a measurable time, their faces impenetrable, their eyes dismissing. So those were Apache women; even their manner of walking was alien.

She identified the Agency, which was one of the smaller structures — she had expected it to be large — and saw the three men sitting. That was surely Ralph on the top step, and by now he must have seen her Ohio license plates and recognized the car, but he did not get up. She felt a sudden anger.

The Agency building stood on the left-hand side of the street. She came to a stop opposite it, on the right. As she did so, the young man rose, came down the steps, and walked to the car, not hurrying. The two older men sat gazing at her. All three faces showed nothing but blankness it was difficult not to read hostility into.

Ralph stopped with his hand on the door. "You got here." The remark was neutral.

She said, "Did I?"

A trace of smile showed about his mouth. "Hard to tell in all this dust. You'd better let me drive; I know these roads, and I can take your car over them with less of a beating than you can."

She was within a hairbreadth of saying "Thanks, I'm going back now," but she didn't, for the same reason that she hadn't turned back at the boundary, and because she remembered how guarded and withdrawn he had been, for all his wings and ribbons, the first time she took him to the country club. She said, "All right," and moved over.

He drove without speaking for nearly five minutes, handling the car carefully and well. Shortly beyond the Agency grounds, the road began to climb. Instead of the hard, dust-yielding baked mud, its surface was of a coarser, reddish earth, less dusty and less dramatically rutted. Scattered cactus and sagebrush on either hand were replaced by occasional piñons and junipers. The land seemed greener; she could not decide whether there was actually more vegetation or whether it was merely that the grass and small plants were not dust-coated and showed up more strongly against the warmer-colored earth.

The cowboy outfit was becoming to him. He was tanned, darker than when she had known him at the base. His nose was high and straight, his lips sculptured, his chin strong. There was the intriguing extra height of his cheekbones, and above them the dark eyes, slightly Oriental. They were not slanted, but at the outer corners of the upper lids there was a fascinating curve. All this was familiar, but the expressionless face remained strange.

They passed a single tall white pine by the side of the

road. As if reaching that point released him, he looked at her and said, "You know, I didn't really believe you'd come until I saw the car." His face had come alive. This was Ralph, after all.

She was astonished to feel so much relief. "I wouldn't have missed it for anything. It isn't everyone who gets formally invited to spend a weekend with Indians."

"My dad was tickled with the whole idea. Mother said I was nuts; she said it would be too strange for you. Still, she's kind of looking forward to it. I think you'll find it interesting."

Of course he had not mentioned the real purpose of her visit, any more than they were able to speak of it between themselves; it mattered so much and seemed so beyond reason. She wondered what that dark Apache mother was thinking, and the sisters — especially the one who had served in the Waves.

He slowed to a stop alongside a pickup truck parked by the road. The driver of the truck wore his hair in braids, heavy ones, the hair black and shiny where it was not wrapped. Ralph had told her once that long-haired Indians were mostly over forty. This one looked middle-aged. He had a blobby big nose in a broad, heavy face. As the two men talked, she thought he seemed a cheerful type.

The language sounded slurred, soft, with a good many "sh" and "l" sounds, punctuated by harsh, throaty consonants. There was a rise and fall of tone. The speech was milder than she had expected, faintly musical, and yet virile. She did not think she could ever hope to understand it.

Presently the man in the truck laughed. Ralph turned to her. "This is my uncle, Juan Grijalva. He and Dad and I run our cattle together."

She smiled at the Indian, who studied her gravely. "You got a gun with you?" he asked.

She saw that his intent was humorous. "No. Do I need one?"

He shook his head. "These Inyans are mighty rough people. And these Inyan veterans, you gotta watch them all the time. You need help, you let out a whoop and I'll come. I gotta keep my nephew in line."

He and Ralph laughed. She didn't think it particularly funny, but she liked the friendliness. She said, "Thanks, I'll remember that."

Ralph said to his uncle, in English, "All right. You'll bring up the salt then?"

"Yeh. Your friend ride?"

Ralph looked at her. She said, "Pretty well — that is, I've been on dude ranches."

Uncle Juan told Ralph, "You pick her out an easy horse, and we can take her along while we set out the salt, and let her view the configuration of the landscape."

As he said the last words, he was watching her closely and his eyes were dancing. Her mouth twitched.

Abruptly, he said, "Well, so long. *Ta'njoh.*"

Ralph said, "*Ta'njoh.*"

Both men started their cars and moved along.

"He took two years at Colorado A. & M.," Ralph told her. "He's really a fine cattleman; I'm learning from him right along. He's my dad's brother, so we kid each other all the time."

"Do uncles and nephews usually kid each other?"

"Only on your father's side. On your mother's side, you use respect. It's the custom."

"Oh." It sounded surprisingly complicated and artificial.

Pines were appearing among the smaller evergreens, and the grass was definitely richer. Presently Ralph said, "Anthropologists call it 'the joking relationship' — I mean relations who kid, like Juan and me. When I marry, he'll kid my wife the same way. It's fun if you're used to it."

For a moment she stiffened, feeling the remark probe toward the central, unmentioned thing, the thing that had seemed possible at the officers' club, at the country club, in the city, and so totally impossible when the young man came down from the steps. She let it pass before speaking the thought that came to her, lest the connection be apparent. "You aren't going back into the Air Force?"

"Not unless they call me back. I belong here. These people are coming up, in the cattle business and a lot of other ways. There are only four of us in the tribe who've been all the way through college, besides maybe half a dozen like Juan, who went part way and then came back. Besides, it's good here. Look at it."

They had never ceased climbing. The air was fresher, the country greener and more rugged. At some distance to their right, a handsome bank of red cliffs paralleled the road, contrasting nicely with the pine and spruce at its base. They came into a long, wide, open meadow on which a score or more of beef cattle were grazing. It was good country.

He asked, "Did you bring a tent, and all?"

"Yes, one of those little green tents, and a cot."

"Good. It's not so long since we lived in tepees, and we're used to being kind of crowded together. There's five of us in the two rooms in Dad's house. You'll be more comfortable in a tent of your own."

When they had driven a little farther, he said, "I'll show

you where I'm laying out my house. After the cattle sales this fall, I'll have enough cash to go ahead and build it. I'm going to put in butane gas for the kitchen, and there's a spring above it, so I can bring water in on straight gravity. I figure on three rooms and a bath to start with, and then build on later. Maybe you can give me some advice. There's good stone handy, as well as lots of timber; I don't know which to build in."

He could not possibly have sounded more casual, nor could she as she answered, "I'd like to see it."

Even so, she was relieved when he started reading brands on the cattle near the road and explaining to her which were good Herefords, which off-color or poorly made. As she already knew, he had delicacy; his capacity for perception and tact had surprised her friends.

Ralph's father's name was Pedro Tanitsin; she must find out, she thought, why Juan had a different surname. Tanitsin had put his house in a fairly narrow, craggy-sided valley with an outlook to the south. It was a simple, small frame house, slightly overdue to be repainted. There were no grounds — that is, no fenced area, smooth grass, or planting of any kind. At the east end of the house was a large, flat-topped shelter, its roof thickly covered with evergreen branches. Beyond that was the bare pole skeleton of a tepee. A heavy truck with a tarpaulin over the hood stood by the house. A hundred feet or so behind it, she made out the horizontal bars of a corral crossing the lines of the ruddy stems of the pines around it and she saw a horse move. Ralph parked the car beside the truck. Two dogs came skulking, but no human being came to meet them.

At the east end of the shelter was a wide opening. When they came to it, Ralph stopped, so she did, too, beside him and a step behind him. Inside were the people — Ralph's father, sitting on a bench, and his mother and his two sisters, standing. There was an interval of silence; she felt awkward, and saw before her the same blank, guarded faces that had repulsed her at the Agency. She was aware of a camp stove, a fire pit in the middle of the floor, some cooking utensils, and a large barrel, in addition to the bench.

Pedro Tanitsin's hair was braided, and he wore a brilliant beadwork vest over a bright flannel shirt, and Levis and moccasins. Ralph's mother wore the native dress; so did the older of his sisters, but instead of wearing her hair loose over her shoulders, she had it clubbed at the back of her neck. That must be Juanita, who had been in the Waves. The other, then, was Mary Ellen. Her hair was bobbed and curled, and she wore one of those gaudy silk blouses servicemen bring back from Japan, and slacks that had never been intended for outdoor life.

The mother spoke a single word, in Apache, and followed it with "Come een." Ralph moved forward, and the girl followed. She felt that she was moving against a wall of rejection. Ralph said something in his own tongue; then, gesturing, "This is my father."

She turned toward him. He nodded once, slowly.

Ralph said, "And this is my mother."

The older woman put out her hand, so the girl took it. The clasp was limp, there was no response to her motion of shaking, and the hand was quickly withdrawn. Then the mother spoke, ending with a laugh.

Ralph said, "She says — Well, you see, a while back one of the government women, some kind of social worker, came here, and she came in talking her head off before anybody had time to get used to her. You came in quietly,

like an Indian. So she says, 'This one has good manners.' "
    The woman laughed again. "Yess, not walk in talkin'."
    The girl felt pleased and relieved. Then she saw that all
of them were smiling except Mary Ellen.
    Juanita gave her a somewhat firmer handclasp and said,
"We were wondering whether you would really come here,
to an Indian camp. I hope you like it." Mary Ellen's touch
was limp and even more fleeting than her mother's; she kept
her eyes down and did not speak.
    It seemed that in summer they lived in the shelter, using
the house only for sleeping and storage. Their housekeeping
was easy and relaxed, rather like a well-organized picnic.
She thought it better not to offer to help with getting supper; instead, she watched and took it easy. Hold back and
go slow, she had decided, were essential elements of Apache
etiquette. Cooking was well advanced when Pedro addressed some commonplace questions to her in heavily
accented English. It was a little as if one of the pines had
decided to speak, and the product, she thought, should have
been less banal.
    They all settled on the ground to eat, in a half circle.
Ralph's mother insisted on giving her an angora skin, dyed
deep blue, to sit on. The food was good, the utensils clean.
In the middle of eating, to which the Indians devoted themselves with very little talk, Mary Ellen said something that
made the others laugh. Juanita interpreted. "She says
Ralph said that you were the kind who would wear Levis and
sit on the earth, and you are."
    She began to see that what she had taken for hostility in
Mary Ellen was defensiveness, just as the inappropriate,
pseudo-elegant costume was. The younger girl had not been
out into the world, like her older brother and sister; nor had

she the self-assurance, the satisfaction with plainly being
Apache, of her parents. Her English was limited and unsteady. The presence of a strange white woman made her
uneasy, and in an Indian, the visitor was beginning to see,
uneasiness takes on the face of guarded enmity.

She herself was beginning to feel at home here. She
looked around her. The incoming night air from beyond
the shelter was chill. A generous fire burned in the central
pit. About her were dark, friendly faces. In the air she
breathed were the smells of smoke, food, coffee, pine
needles, and the near-perfume of juniper boughs that had
been brought up from lower county to make the walls of
the shelter thicker and more fragrant. It was incredible that
she should be here at this moment, stirring the sugar in a
fresh cup of coffee, listening to the musical rise and fall of
a woman's voice saying something in that mysterious
tongue. She looked sidelong at Ralph. In the shifting, red-
dened firelight, he was darker, at once familiar, loved, and
alien, primitive. Could it be possible, after all? Was it anything more than a remnant of a madness that had seized
her when she went visiting a friend who had married a
fly-boy major?

By the end of the third day she had to remind herself that
all this was as strange as it was. Ralph planned to build a
modern house, but the family's half-camping mode of life
was agreeable; come winter, though, the inside of that little
house would be on the grim side. The family were friendly,
easy to be with, especially once Mary Ellen, feeling secure,
had returned to native costume.

They had a radio, which they listened to chiefly for news,
weather, and cattle price reports, Ralph or Juanita translat-
ing for their parents. Mary Ellen read movie magazines.

Juanita dipped into textbooks that would help her in college (the University of New Mexico had accepted her for next fall) and, for the same purpose, was struggling through Vanity Fair. The white woman was able to help her there, realizing as she did so what a staggeringly broad context an educated white person moved and thought in, learned without effort, all of which an Indian had to grasp item by item. To speak English, read, and write was only the beginning.

Ralph and Uncle Juan, who visited daily, went in for bulletins from the extension service and agricultural colleges, reading them and then expounding their contents to Pedro. She was amused by the automatic gesture with which Uncle Juan would brush a braid back when it fell on the page. She had thought she had learned a little of the cattle business on a dude ranch near Tucson, where they made a big thing of running beef stock; not until now had she imagined it could be a bookish vocation with a highly technical vocabulary. Ralph and Juan turned to her to verify the meaning of "it is a far cry from," and in the same sentence were two words they had to explain to her. This amused Pedro greatly; he didn't know much English, but he had learned those.

Reading was occasional and in the daytime. After dinner, in the firelit dark, they told stories. Pedro, it turned out, was a noted storyteller in his own language. He talked and Ralph translated and explained. The stories had quality, and through them she saw that the Apaches, too, had a considerable context to be learned.

In her cot that night, with the sweet, cold air on her cheek, hearing the shushing rise and fall of a soft breeze in the high pines, she thought that it was possible, it could happen. It was just possible. Ralph in the saddle was magnificent. Uncle Juan sat his horse like a rock that had become one with the animal, but Ralph was fine-waisted live whalebone. They were fun to ride with — considerate, instructive, humorous.

As they went about the range, there was nothing that moved, nothing out of place, that they did not see, at the farthest distance to which good eyes could reach. They made no apparent effort, she was not conscious that they were scouting, but they saw everything and were not content until it was explained. A pinto horse, an over-age steer with long horns — whose? A truck, two mounted men — to her, when she finally made them out, no more than dots on a distant road — who were they? Where were they going?

It made her think of bygone days and Apaches on the warpath. Some of those warriors had still been alive when Ralph was a boy. The warpath training had not been dropped. It made her think, as well, of Ralph high in the air alongside the Yalu, and his record of kills. There was a closer link between a deadly grandfather with a painted face and the skilled pilot than one would have thought.

Nothing was quite what she had expected, and least expected of all was the constant thread of laughter — the happy Indian laughter running through everything, so light and so easily provoked. And it was possible, just barely possible — that is, if *they* accepted *her*. Before she came here, she had not thought of that. What was definite was that she was in love with Ralph. When she had fully faced that, tired as she was, she was long in falling asleep.

The following afternoon, Ralph told her, "There's a neighbor of ours had a curing ceremony a while back. What he had was a virus and a touch of pneumonia, and they cured that at the hospital, but he had a sing, too. They do that a lot. There's something to it; the doctor takes care of the physical end, and the medicine man takes care of the psychosomatic. Anyway, now he has to 'pick up' the ceremony, as they say. It's a kind of thanksgiving. He puts up a tepee, and they make *tulapai* — that's a kind of beer made from corn. The neighbors come in, and there's a little singing and a feast, and we drink *tulapai* and talk, then at the end everybody gets blessed."

She said, "It sounds interesting. Do they get drunk?"

"You'd have to work hard to get drunk on *tulapai*. It just makes everybody happy. While you're seeing the Apaches, you ought to see this, only — Well, it's kind of unsanitary. They fill a lard pail and pass it around. Of course, you're not an Indian, so it will be all right if you want to use a cup."

"I don't think that's necessary."

Ralph was pleased. "All right. Anyway, it will be just us and Uncle Juan's family, and this man's — his name is Pablo Horses. They're all healthy, and they're clean."

Near sundown, they drove the mile to Pablo's place in her car and the truck. That was her first sight of a real-life tepee; she was struck by its symmetry, the way in which the curved canvas caught the light, and the effect of the long, sloping white line against a green background. Inside, the tepee seemed even roomier than it had looked from the outside.

The door faced east. In the middle, there was a small, fragrant fire, and a kerosene lantern hung near the host's place at the back. The men sat on the south, the women on the north. All of them were wearing elements of Indian costume — items of buckskin, beadwork, Navajo silver, and

Pueblo turquoise and shell. Pedro had his beaded vest on again; she knew now that his donning it that first day had been in honor of her. Ralph had put a wide band of beadwork around his hat, and at his throat, instead of his cowboy's scarf, he wore a broad choker of elk bone and beads. It was becoming.

All of them had blankets. Juanita had insisted that she take one, and had given her a handsome, soft, expensive Pendleton. The idea of wearing it had embarrassed her, but now she felt that it helped her to blend in. She'd turn into an Apache yet, she thought.

Their host, a craggy man with definitely gray hair, was older than Pedro Tanitsin. Because this was a ceremony, he had an eagle feather tied to the top of his head.

All of them, and especially the women, were amused that a white woman should come to drink *tulapai*. There were comments and laughter. Juanita, sitting next to her, said, "You mustn't mind. It's good. You are giving people a good feeling, so that helps what we are doing."

Pablo Horses took up a rattle and began a chant, in which the older men joined. The time was slow and monotonous, the music narrow in range, and heavy. It was dull, and yet, as the girl listened, the monotonous rhythm and droning voices took hold of her. There was a curious power there.

After four songs, Pablo's daughter brought in a pail of *tulapai*, which was passed around solemnly, clockwise. Unsanitary, certainly; the girl wished she had asked for a cup, but they did seem a healthy lot. The drink itself was good, like beer but with a fresh quality that suggested hard cider. There were four more sets of four songs each, with a circuit of the pail after each set, and then the business of sprinkling a yellow powder and brushing the air with feathers. Everyone had sat still during the chant; the refreshment period was a break, when people changed positions. Pablo's women brought in food. The girl felt no noticeable lift from the small amount of the beer she had taken, but it did seem to have sharpened her appetite.

When they had eaten, Pablo said, "Young lady, where you come from?"

She said, "Ohio — Cleveland."

A young man, Uncle Juan's son, said, "I was there one time when I was in the Army. They got a good U.S.O." That took care of Cleveland.

An elderly man — Pablo's brother, she believed — asked, "How you like it here?"

"I like it. This is beautiful country."

Ralph took the trouble to translate that. Pablo said, "Yess. This is our country, Apache country." Then he went on at some length in Apache.

Juanita explained, "He's taken what you said as a kind of text, and he's telling how this is our country, and we must keep it, and we must live up to our Apache traditions."

More *tulapai* was brought in. The women were speaking up more than usual. There was an atmosphere of geniality and relaxation, but no ugliness, nothing one could call drunkenness.

The man she believed to be Pablo's brother, after a good draught of beer, launched upon a long story. Soon someone laughed. A little later, they all laughed. There were interruptions of laughter all through the latter part of the narration.

When he had finished, Ralph translated. "This is Tomás Horses speaking. He lives about five miles from here, and in between Pablo's place and his there is a place called Yellow Spring, where people camp. That's important.

"He says there is a Pueblo Indian called Malaquias he knows pretty well, a smart trader. Three or four times, when Tomás has visited that Pueblo, Malaquias has given him wine, then traded with him when he was high, and outsmarted him. So he's been waiting for a chance to get even."

They were all listening eagerly. Hearing the story a second time, knowing the point, made it all the more delightful.

"Well, about a week ago Malaquias came trading jewelry, and he camped at Yellow Spring. Tomás had some whiskey, so he made his plan. He came and borrowed Pablo's buckskin; that's a fast, strong horse and hard to hold once he gets going."

There were giggles.

"Then he drove to Yellow Spring in his wagon and told this man, 'My friend, put your goods in my wagon and come to my house. I'll give you a drink, and you can have supper with me, and perhaps we can do a little business.' "

This, it seemed, was hilarious.

"So he went along, and Tomás poured whiskey for him." More laughter. "Tomás went light. All the same, they traded, and the Pueblo traded him out of that buckskin for that string of turquoise he's wearing. The poor Apache had been gypped again." Ralph's own voice shook as he said this.

"So he gave the man some more whiskey, and kept him there for supper. Meantime, his two boys — this one here and another one, who's away now — went down the road about a mile and strung wire across between two trees."

The punctuations of laughter were almost continuous.

"So Tomás gave Malaquias a hackamore for the buckskin, and Malaquias started for his camp after dark, and good and tight. The buckskin was headed toward home, you understand, and Malaquias could not stop him when he started running. So they came to that wire, and it took him just right, under the chin, and threw him right off the horse. The horse came on back to Pablo's."

The telling had to stop for seconds of laughter.

"Then Tomás and the boys went and got the wire, and he sent this boy to the ranger station to tell how there was this foreign Indian lying in the road with his neck all torn and they'd better pick him up. By and by, they picked him up and took him to the hospital. He's still there."

Ralph looked about him, chuckling over the humor of it, feeling the successful narrator's glow. His audience was given over to laughter — all but the girl he loved, who seemed somehow alien, remote, so that he was unusually conscious of her paleness. He caught Juanita's eye, and she threw back her head to laugh again. Then he looked at the girl once more. She was so still, her eyes fixed on the ground. Wanting her to share in this as she had in so much else these last days, he forgot his satisfaction with his performance and studied her with concern, trying to reach what was in her mind, what was the matter. At that moment, she raised her eyes and looked directly at him. The last traces of pleasure left his face, because, as he read her now, her thoughts all laid open, he knew that this had ended it, and that she would start home the first thing tomorrow.

The Brush of
the Wings

THE SEASON, GERALD THOUGHT, WAS
strangely loaded with death. But he had learned enough
about himself to suspect that the fact that he thought this
— that he was so conscious of the cumulative oppression of
his personal losses and the public news — might mean his
imagination was about to play a trick on him, the trick he
privately called "going through the door."

Gerald was more than on the threshold of success, and
within the next ten years was sure to become a partner in
the law firm in which he was an associate. In prep school
and college, he had hoped and wanted more than anything
else to become a poet — a hope he did not give up until he
was well into his thirties, when the grind of law school and
his long drudgeries as a junior associate in a big law firm
had all but put a stop to the writing he had kept up industriously until then. Later on, as the nature of his work
changed and became more intense, more responsible, but
less merely burdensome, he had been able to set aside quiet

time — whole evenings, Sundays — for writing. In this his
wife, Clara, encouraged him. For several years, he hoped
once again for what he described to himself as the brush of
the wings, uncertain whether he meant of an angel, of inspiration, or of a muse. About the time their son was born,
with a conscious sense of affectionate, indulgent amusement
toward the romantic youth he had once been, Gerald gave
up his literary ambition. The wings would never brush him.
Not for him the enchanting or the piercing verse; his best
work would be the clear, cogent prose of briefs — which, he
held, were a form of art, and Clara agreed with him.

A considerable part of the work of such firms as the one
Gerald was associated with lies in reading the future — fore-
casting what, under given circumstances, a state or federal
commission is likely to decide, what the decision in a pend-
ing case may be, and what effect this or that decision and
its later applications might have on the activities of the
firm's clients, or how governmental agencies might view a
proposed venture. Upon the correctness of these predic-
tions depend hundreds of millions of dollars. The final
predicting, usually styled "advice," is done by the firms'
partners. A junior associate's business is largely endless research, but even the lowliest of them should be able to
organize the data he amasses in relation to the desired whole
and to spot the particularly significant items. Gerald made
one bad slip during his junior period. It was in a minor
matter, involving the probable outcome of a case then being
tried, which was important to him just because it *was* minor,
since he was allowed to handle it entirely by himself, up to
the point of submitting to one of the partners of the firm a
draft of the advice Gerald thought the client should be
given. The judge before whom the case was being tried was

atrabilious and had shown personal convictions in other cases about subjects that came into the arguments on this one. From this, Gerald concluded that the judge, in his thinking, would take a certain initial position, and that led Gerald himself to arrive, by a tight, smooth, logical sequence, at a final decision that required advising the firm's client to abandon its proposal. The partner who passed on his work said it was beautiful and, in a legal way, read like something by Poe. He told Gerald that caution, even an element of pessimism, was highly desirable, but one should not be led into false assumptions on that side any more than on the side of optimism. In this case, while Gerald's estimate of certain fallibilities in the judge's makeup was not inaccurate, he had assumed that the judge would make certain findings that any judge would know that any court of appeals would reject. Gerald did his work over in such a manner as to earn himself a word of definite approval.

He knew privately what had happened: He had "gone through the door." It began in prep school, when his civics class had been taken through several mills and a power plant. The power plant, with its linked dynamos, beautiful, almost musical, cleanly logical, had enchanted him. The mills — the machines moving jerkily and going clackety-clack, and the people who tended them moving to the machine's unrhythm, not going clackety-clack audibly but, he was sure, in their souls — he had hated. That night he wrote a sonnet on the dynamos, and it had turned out well. Then, though much too tired, he tried to write about the factories, and got tangled up in reminiscences of "The Song of the Shirt," gave up and went to bed, and dreamed that he went through the door into a mill. On either side of him, machines stretched away to the end of a very long hall. The machines had the quiet and beauty of dynamos, but they were assembly lines. They seemed as unattended as dynamos are, but he knew that slaves he could not see were moving about them. From machine to machine passed the thing they manufactured, which was something that should not be made. The machines impelled him and their product down the hall toward a farther door. Beyond that waited death and destruction. He waked, of course, before he went through it. The nightmare was all the more terrible because it was accompanied by a sense of perfection and beauty.

The dream recurred only twice, and in blurred form, but he soon saw that there were times when, awake, he was subject to a kind of logic of disaster — when, having accepted the initial premise, he was drawn on through to an acceptance of the idea of defeat. His faulty analysis of that case had taught him that this trick of the imagination, this — so to speak — "going through the door" into the mill of his nightmare, could crop up in his law work and that it behooved him to guard against it. Hence, in that later season of deaths and news of deaths, he was wary of his own thought processes.

In choosing a wife, he could hardly have done better than Clara. She was slim, high-colored, fine-featured, with dark hair, long, dark lashes, and very blue eyes. He himself was well made, solid, on the fair side, and pleasant-looking. They made a good couple. She was both likable and lovable. She was aesthetically sensitive, she was perceptive where her husband was concerned, and she stood behind him.

Her first pregnancy ended in an unpleasant failure, from which it took her some time to recover. Three years later, she produced a boy. There could be no more, but the one was triumphant. The child grew. He was not precocious, but he was intelligent, cheerful, friendly. He had imagination. That it was anything more than the unfettered imaging natural to any child, that here were the makings of a real writer, Gerald refused to think.

If he himself had ever had a successful creation, it was the boy, who, as he passed his second and then his third birthday, lighted their household. He was the source of endless trouble, and both his parents wondered how they had supported the empty years before he came — much as Gerald, in those years, had wondered how he had supported the vacancy of life without Clara. The child seemed to be inheriting his mother's looks and his father's build — an excellent union of grace and strength. Gerald was incapable of the dullness of thinking of him as totally a product of himself, as a poem would be, or as a product of himself and Clara. Here was an individual, a third person. He might have inherited this physical feature and that mental gift, but he was making himself; he was infinitely more than a product. This individuality, this clearly defined singleness of a person in his own right, induced humility, but it did not at all lessen the satisfaction and delight of having been in some measure the author of its being, or of the sense of mutual possession between himself and his son.

Through their separate relationships with the child, the parents found their own relationship perfected. Family life gained intensity and a sense of constant newness. Gerald wondered at times how many of his colleagues and friends, in appearance as conformingly ordinary as Clara and he, lived with an equal, private excitement. It occurred to him occasionally, at certain moments with his son, when the simple fact of his nature and being as a child seemed overwhelming, that through him he came nearer than he ever had through his writing to knowing what the brush of the wings was like — the wings of terror and of exaltation.

When the boy was three and a half, in June, shortly after they had moved to the country for the summer, Gerald's cousin Martha died. Her death was not unexpected; she had been seriously ill for some time. They had seen each other only occasionally since they grew up, and their correspondence had seldom gone beyond an exchange of longish letters at Christmas, but they had been close as children, they communicated warmly and frankly, and her going left him without a single close relative. There was a code he would never use again. There were mental associations that hereafter he would be able to mention to no one.

It was after that that he became conscious of the depressing character of the daily news. He was unsure whether, in fact, they had entered one of those extra-unpleasant periods that occur from time to time, or whether the change was in his sensitivity to what he read. He thought of making a back check of the papers for the month before his cousin's death, but did not get around to it. Israel and her neighbors were busy shooting up each other's outposts and border settlements, French North Africa was all battle and rapine, and there were riots, stonings of consulates, burnings of houses, in a dozen countries. At home, the governor of the state had launched a big drive for safety on the highways, in co-operation with which the newspapers played up fatal accidents for all they were worth.

Then one of those same accidents claimed the life of Todd Hopkins, Gerald's most intimate friend. Todd and he had gone to the same prep school and had liked each other there. They had chosen different colleges and law schools, and then been reunited in Gerald's law firm. After a lapse of years, old school connections often prove false, even slightly embarrassing, because they no longer have meaning and yet the wearers of the tie feel called upon to keep making gestures as if they did. In the case of Gerald and Todd, however, the old association proved valid. They became fonder of each other year by year. Latterly they had worked together a good deal, and in the firm were recognized as an effective team. Gerald was the more brilliant, the one who would first become a partner. Todd had more humor. He was more relaxed under pressure. He had sweetness enough to show that he admired his friend, which was warming. It gave Gerald a sense of comfort and steadiness to work with Todd. He had even felt close enough to him to tell him about the phenomenon of going through the door, and at least once Todd had spotted a line of pessimistic reasoning in Gerald's work that sprang from it.

His cousin's death had left Gerald with a feeling of mild loneliness, of a lid closed on part of the past, a fixture gone from his horizon. The snatching of Todd out of his world tore a hole in it. After a day or two, he was confronted with the fact that in time the edges would cease to be jagged, but the hole would never entirely be filled. Clara had not known Todd well; the Hopkinses lived year round in New Jersey, while she and Gerald had chosen Manhattan, with a rented house at the seashore in summer. For all her real sympathy, Gerald could not quite share his memory or his loss with her, but fell back instead into a lonely internal dialogue with himself.

Todd Hopkins was killed in August. A week after the funeral, a nasty virus swept through the combination play school and infant swimming class that the boy went to three days a week, and he, too, came down with it. The virus got its work in during a spell of northeasterly weather that kept the children indoors. Its course was predictable. It ran about a week, with several days of really high fever, stomach ache, and generalized aches and pains. Toward the end, there were likely to be nosebleeds. The local pediatrician was excellent. He told Clara what to expect; it was an unpleasant business but no cause for fear. All the same, it is thoroughly upsetting to feel one's child furiously hot with fever, to have him crying from what medical people call "discomfort," and to be unable to quiet him even with the proven magic of holding and rocking him.

On Wednesday evening, when Gerald came home, Clara told him with intense relief that the boy's temperature had dropped. He had eaten some gelatin. Gerald took a turn with him. He was cheerful, but unnaturally quiet. You could see how the child had lost weight; his eyes, as blue as his mother's, were too large for his face. His father thought him too beautiful, alarmingly so.

He had a nosebleed early Thursday morning. It was Clara who first heard his frightened call and went in to him. She was pretty well worn out by the days just past, and the sight of the rich bleeding was too much for her. Gerald took over, fully prepared to be late, to miss a morning or a day from work. He managed to get his son interested in the idea of the little pipes through which blood runs, one of which had broken and had to get well, and got him past the fear. He sold him on the cracked ice. The bleeding stopped soon enough for Gerald to eat breakfast at the usual time. He felt wrung out and was surprised at his appetite. He told Clara to telephone the doctor on general principles, as soon as he could be reached at his office, and went to work.

When Gerald came home that night, he found that there had been three more nosebleeds, none as severe as the first. Clara had dealt with them competently. She was haggard, and he began to worry lest she catch the bug, too. He took his turn with the boy. The fever had stayed down, although the child's face was still flushed. He ate some junket. Then he grew sleepy, and his father left him about seven. He did not think there would be more bleeding.

Gerald and Clara had a cocktail and ate dinner. Gerald prescribed a glass of claret apiece.

Shortly after eight, they went into the boy's room, found him drowsily awake, and gave him an aspirin tablet, the pink, lemony-tasting kind you have to hide lest children eat it as candy. It was important that he have it, to keep his fever down and insure his sleep. They also took his temperature, and were relieved that it was a hundred degrees even. Clara was easier than she had been when her husband came home, but still tense, and plainly done in. He told her to take a sleeping pill and go to bed; he had brought some work with him and would tackle that and listen for the boy. She resisted for no good reason, and then suddenly, gladly, gave in.

Gerald took his work up to the guest room, and left the door open and the nursery door open a crack. He set up a bridge table and started in on his papers. He was just well lost in the reading when the boy cried out. Gerald got up and went in to him, closing the nursery door and switching on a shaded, fifteen-watt bulb he had put into a fixture when the sickness started.

It was another nosebleed, not a bad one, but the boy must have been asleep and the blood had run into his throat, partly choking him, and he was frightened. Gerald's first concern was to quiet him. Clara's pill would be just about taking effect and he did not want her wakened. He and the boy rocked together in the rocking chair. It was an old chair with an irritating squeak to which his son was devoted. Clara had put a refilled ice bag in the washbasin in the bathroom, just in case. When the boy was calm, Gerald was able to leave him, sitting in the chair and holding Kleenex to his nose, long enough to run and get it. What a good little soldier the kid was, Gerald thought with a sudden, purely male pride as he came back to him; what a little man when the pinch came. He took the boy on his lap again, and, rocking, set a fold of the ice bag against the infantile little nose. The coolness of the bag in his hand made him sharply aware of the warmth of the room, which he found uncomfortable. The boy pushed the ice bag gently aside, leaned forward, and spat out a small amount of blood, which landed on Gerald's knee. Gerald reached for the tissues, wiped his knee, and set the ice bag in place again as the small head went back against the crook of his elbow. The incident struck him as funny. He took the piece of tissue the child had been holding, which showed a trace of blood, and gave him a fresh one.

The boy said softly, "Too much cold," and Gerald set the bag on the floor. The hand in which the boy had been holding the fresh Kleenex to his nose lowered slowly; the paper was unspotted. Both his hands went limp and his eyes closed. His body relaxed all over. Gerald had heard and read of children going to sleep in their parents' arms, and had been disappointed that it almost never happened with him; the child was too live, too determined not to miss anything. Gerald felt a deep satisfaction now.

After a moment or two, he felt the child's neck. It was cool; it seemed much cooler than the room. He felt the hands, and the ankles between the snug cuffs of the pajamas and the slippers; they were chilly. Making a long arm, he got a blanket from the bed. He kept on rocking, hearing at each backward swing the unfriendly creak of the chair. He could see well by the weak bulb now; but around everything, and especially around the boy's face, was an overlay of shadow. You could hardly tell that he was breathing. He looked pale, but that could be the light. Gerald had never seen that face so limp. There were traces of blood around the nostril that had bled, and below both nostrils a little blood at the corners of the mouth, which had fallen open. The dark lashes lay on the cheeks, and the shadow over the eyelids.

Of course the aspirin, which to an infant of that age was a powerful drug, had taken effect, all the more strongly for having been held off. You would expect the child to be exhausted. The nosebleeds had been predicted and were not excessive. Gerald himself felt cold, although he was still conscious of the warmth of the room. As the child reclined, his head slightly back, his nostrils were more important than usual in his face. They had an extraordinary quality of slackness; so had his lips, as though the outlines of lips and nostrils had been fudged in the drawing. Limp, a pervasive limpness, the eyelids and lashes, the nose, the mouth, the whole body. He wanted to lift the blanket and look at the hands, but could not. Those hands moved him too much. He had thought it funny when the boy spat blood, but perhaps it was not. Where had that blood come from? For a moment he felt himself swirl and sink.

There were two impossibilities. One was to perform any act that did not belong in the normal process of quieting a child; the other was to awaken Clara. He went on rocking slowly. It was all very well that the various stages of this illness had been predicted by the doctor; there is always the exception. What are the effects of a hundred and four degrees of fever, not in the evening but on waking in the morning? He had entered the chain of reasoning along which he had to follow, knowing that it led in perfect beauty to an end from which somehow he must turn aside before he reached it. A detached part of his mind stated clearly that this was pure emotion, tinged with an almost literary element, but that recognition was theoretical and ineffectual. Somewhere he had seen a face like this depicted. Or was it carved? Painted, he thought. He had an unplaceable memory of a picture of deathly relaxation. At the time, it had seemed just bad, gruesome realism.

He set himself to rock a hundred times, counting. His heart was beating too hard and too fast, in a way that was alarming in itself and that aroused an ancient, feral certainty of danger. His stomach was moist; there was sweat on his cold palms. Eighteen, nineteen, twenty . . . His solitude was unutterable, but that was required as he moved along the silent links of fear. There was nothing to do but wait and find out, and it was for him alone. The child did not stir. Thirty-five, thirty-six, thirty-seven . . . There are wings in the room now, he thought bitterly — the dreadful wings of the dark angel. He needed Clara to the center of his bowels, and he thanked God she was not there. The thought of the doctor never occurred to him. His counting reached fifty. By then, he knew how close Todd was to all this, and behind him Martha and all the season's accumulation of death; but above all these was Todd — not as an emissary, not as an enemy, but part of the linkage.

At the seventy-sixth rock of the chair, the boy let his head fall over, so his cheek lay on Gerald's arm. At ninety-one, he snored once, and thereafter his breathing was strong and moderately audible. With a giddy desire for laughter, Gerald realized that, throughout the counting, his son's body had been snugly warm against his. The seventeenth-century practice of blood-letting, he thought with an inclination to giggle, combined with aspirin, would produce a low temperature.

He tucked the sleeping infant into bed, stood for a moment to watch and listen, and then left the room. He felt weak and as if he had been cleansed throughout his body. He went downstairs, mixed a whiskey-and-soda, and settled down with the drink and a smoke. The documents could go for this evening. In half an hour he would check on the boy and go to bed. He felt as if he had just completed a very important, difficult piece of work. He felt extraordinarily at ease. He looked at his watch. He would wait a full thirty minutes before looking in on his son, although he was magnificently sleepy.

Spud and
Cochise

TOO MUCH LIGHT — TOO MUCH HEAT, TOO
much sand and rock, but above all too much light made
the desert intolerable, the brilliance striking everything to
whiteness. Not the dead white of a painted board, but
shades and variations, yellowish in a pale way over some of
the sand, in other places greenish, rocks that might turn out
purple if the sun went behind a cloud, mesas that might
have red in their sides. The faint tones were mineral, weak
but still harsh. What vegetation managed to live, cactus
and yucca and little enough of it, was also pale and ineffectual.

In the still air, the strawberry roan's hoofs stirred up a
powdery dust-haze at each step, the fine stuff rose, covering
legs and flanks and mane until the animal became a uniform,
pinkish gray, it settled on Spud's spurs, his boots, his rifle
in its scabbard, his threadbare blue jeans, his pistol, his
cotton shirt, the yellow silk scarf at his throat, his straggly
mustache, his leather face, and battered, wide hat. Spud

was a small, pepper-and-salt man anyhow, now he looked like a flour sack with nothing in it.

He was too dry to smoke or sing, too disciplined to let his mind run on drinks. He made himself easy in the saddle, forebore to count the miles that still lay between himself and Spareribs, and tried to occupy himself by observing the Mil Huesos desert. This was not interesting, especially since he had seen it all before. It took some thought to follow the trail. In many sandy stretches there was nothing to follow. Where the footing turned to what looked like cosmic cinders, or where it went over rock, there was a thin ribbon of special texture, something hardly visible, but which to Spud proclaimed the road. Alongside it he noted a scattering of dung on one place. That's the nearest thing to company I've had in two days, he thought. He watched it slide by him as the roan maintained his fast, monotonous, mile-eating walk. He lifted his hat an inch to cool his head, shifted his revolver to a better position, and settled even more slackly in the saddle.

A long, low, white ridge with greenish shading on its upper part ran out to a point a short distance ahead. That was where he would hit the main trail. He looked at the ridge, then over to the western mountains, a pile of stone skeletons, bluish without promise of growth or coolness, on the horizon, then back to the earth nearby. The bones of a horse came into view. I'll bet you was a godsend to the ants in this district, he thought.

A pillar of dust, like to his own but broader, rose from behind the ridge, moving slowly to meet his course. He touched the handle of his gun while he looked at it. Two horses, or a rider and a packhorse. Might be company. Someone coming from Spareribs. His gray eyes became

careful, the dust-filled wrinkles about them drawing together.

Just at the end of the point the dust-cloud stopped,
thinned, faded away. Spud became more watchful. Things
that go out of sight, that act differently, require caution. He
loosed the carbine in its scabbard, set himself almost
straight in the saddle, and shortened his reins slightly.

He was near the point now. Over its low top he saw two
horses, one saddled, one packed. As he cleared it he saw a
person — a woman, for God's sake — sitting in the shade
of her horse, hunched up, looking gloomy. She was all
dust, too, her and her print shirt and divided skirt; from a
little distance you couldn't tell anything about her barring
that she was white.

Curious, Spud turned the roan toward her. A shotgun
was slung from her saddle horn by a female arrangement
of strings. She raised her head slightly, watching him coming without interest or friendliness. Her animals were
poor, they stood with low heads at the end of hollow necks,
their manes were heavy with dust. He stopped a few
yards from her, raised his hat and said, "Good evenin',
ma'am."

"Evenin'." Her voice was neutral, her eyes ungreeting.

Curiosity still urged. "Hot, ain't it?"

"Yeah. It's hot. That's what this country's for."

"That's right."

Spud untied his canteen. "Could you use a drink o'
water? I'd be pleased if you'd join me, ma'am."

She smiled unexpectedly, as at a sour joke. "Thanks,
yes."

He moved his horse nearer, reached down the canteen of
more than tepid water, and watched her drink sparingly.

"I'm headin' for Spareribs," he said, bringing himself as near to inquiry as courtesy would allow.

"I'm headin' *from* Spareribs." She stressed the "from." After a pause, as though to make up for needless rudeness, she said, "I'm hittin' for Tucson and I figure to camp at Ojo Amarillo."

Spud glanced at the sun, well past noon, and said, "If you'll pardon me, ma'am, you must ha' started kind o' late. I don't think you can make Oja Amarillo today. I — I kind o' think maybe you'd do better if you come back to Spareribs and make a nice, early start tomorrow. You'd make it easy then."

"Thank you. I ain't goin' back to Spareribs."

"Yes'm." Spud felt rebuked. "Excuse me havin' interfered. I guess I'll be goin' along." He lifted his rein hand, then hesitated, looking again at the woman's face. Hard to make out under the dust, youngish anyway, familiar . . .

"I'll beg you to excuse me again. It jest kind o' seems to me I seen you somewheres before."

She sighed, then smiled slightly with one corner of her mouth. "Likely you have," she said indifferently. "Was you ever to the Golden Girl in Tucson?"

Spud was taken completely aback, unseated to the extent of saying, "Oh, are you — " before he could check himself.

"Yeah, I am." She wiped her mouth hard with the back of her hand and looked at it. "I was, anyway, and I guess I will be again. Right now it seems to have worn off."

Spud heard the humility, the sound of despair. He fumbled for words. He could think of nothing delicate, and finally came out flat with what moved in him.

"Can I help you any ways at all?"

She stared at him, curiosity, distrust, a little wonder. "I don't reckon. I'm hooked, I guess. Earmarked."

Another pause followed. Spud took out the makings. "Will you have a smoke with me, ma'am?"

"All right."

He passed the makings down, then rolled himself one. He reached low with his match. The Indians are right about tobacco. The two smokes lit from a common flame, of herb from one sack, started a friendlier circuit between them.

She said, "I kind of remember you. You busted Buckskin Smith out the window."

"That was me."

"We was grateful to you. He was real ugly."

They smoked awhile in silence.

"I'll tell you," she said. "It'll do me good, and you're a nice kind of man. I don't mind tellin' you.

"I saved up some money, and I bought up the Dead Soldier Mine in Spareribs, figurin' it would pay all right as soon as the Apaches was chased away. Well, they been chased, for a while, anyhow, so I packed up and come out to Spareribs to work it. Do you know Snakeweed?"

"I do."

"Well, he's settled in Spareribs. He's got Spareribs and he's got my mine. So he tells me, if I want to work it, I can marry him. Snakeweed!" Spud nodded. "There's limits to what a girl can take. So I'm headin' back. I tried to get out o' the corral, but I guess it's too high for me."

Spud studied her again. Young, definitely young under hard lines, bitterness, and dirt. Still a girl. He shifted uneasily. He'd made up his mind to his age, he was through with trouble. Still a girl, and wants to live nice.

She spoke again, relieving pain. "I figured there wouldn't be no one know me in Spareribs; I figured I could make a nice livin' off of that mine and by and by marry somebody.

Yessir, that's what I figured. Only you couldn't marry Snakeweed, could you?"

"I never thought about him just that way, ma'am, but I guess not — no, he wouldn't hardly do."

"Well, I guess it's all right. I guess a girl like me ain't got no call tryin' to marry. It ain't on the cards."

"Don't you believe it, ma'am. Don't let 'em tell you that. Listen, I've been around some. I'm a quiet man, barrin' when I'm mad, but I didn't grow old settin' still. I've seen plenty. And some mighty fine wives come out of where you been." Spud paused. "Can you cook?"

"I can cook. I can make a flapjack the size o' the fryin' pan and so light you got to be careful breathin' or it'll blow away. I can make a lemon pie that if you're settin' out on the front porch, your mouth'll water when I take it out o' the oven. I can make beans you'd swear was strawberries."

Spud nodded. "Them's qualifications." He shifted in the saddle. Trouble again. Back at it. "Listen to me, ma'am. Don't you go to Tucson. About five mile down the trail you'll see a yaller mesa. You take the left fork, and by and by you go down into Alamos Canyon, and then you hit Alamos. It ain't much of a place, but it's all right. You go to the Bon Ton Hotel and Eatin' House — you can't miss it, it's nigh on to all there is — and ask for Hank Stromberg. Tell Hank I sent you and that you're to wait for me there. He'll take care o' you. He might give you a job waitin', if you wanted it. I'll take care o' Snakeweed."

"That's nice o' you, mister, but I don't think it'll work. I've read my cards, and that's what my hand says."

Spud swung himself sideways and raised his right hand, shaking it once at her. "I'm Spud Flynn," he said. "I'm a half-blood Irish on my father's side and I come of a race o' kings; I know things more than what you just see. I know what's in the draw you ain't picked up yet, and I ordain that you wait for me at Hank's."

That was a good word, ordain, he thought, and wondered where he got it from.

The expression of her face changed slightly, became less hard. "But you can't handle Snakeweed. No offense, Mr. Flynn, but he's tough. It calls for an awful big man, and a hard one, and one with power, to get Snakeweed. You might get hurt."

"It ain't just size. I'll tell you, Miss — "

"Hartshorn, Elvira Hartshorn."

"Thank you, Miss Hartshorn. Well, this'll make it clear to you. I was in an awful hurry once. I'd rode my horse down and I was pushin' along on foot with reason to get further. I struck a dry wash, too wide to jump, too steep to climb down. I was stuck. This was up in the Black Hills. And an eagle come by, and I roped him. He kept a-swingin' back and forth, tryin' to get loose, and when he was swingin' good, I jumped with him and we went acrost. It cost me a good maguey rope, but it worked fine. Well, that's what I mean. A heavier man couldn't ha' done it. It ain't all size. Nor I ain't fixin' to get myself hurt none."

"I guess you know yourself. I sure appreciate your tryin', Mr. Flynn."

"You can expect me in about — well — a week from tomorrow."

"Thursday week?"

"Thursday? You shore keep track. I kind o' thought it was Monday, but I hadn't really noticed. Thursday week, then."

She rose and they shook hands. "I'm pleased to have met you, Miss Hartshorn."

"I'm pleased to know you, Mr. Flynn. Wait a minute;

I got something for you. It ain't much, but it's — well — something to show I appreciate what you're doin'."

From her saddle bags she took two peculiar flat, blue bottles. Spud's eyes widened.

"Take them along," she said, "they might be handy, or comfortin'."

Spud knew the form of those bottles from dim memory. Four-Eye Monongahela, liquor so good even barkeeps can't help drinking it, so rare that only twice in his life had he ever tasted it. Two bottles! Just thinking about them, he felt the springs of his old youth welling inside him. It's so long since I really been drunk, he thought, drunk like a hero.

"Thank you kindly, Miss Hartshorn," he said, lifting his hat. "Well, I'll be seein' you Thursday week. *Hasta la vista.*"

"Take care o' yourself."

The roan raised its head, awoke, felt injured, knew the spurs and returned to its fast, somnambulistic walk. The dust rose around them again, the little rocks and changes of kinds of sand and ineffectual cactus growths slid by, dropped behind. A man needs a hatbrim under his chin, Spud thought, feeling the heat strike upward from the desert. Saves shavin'; all my whiskers is sizzled off.

And I'm through with gettin' drunk like a hero. Hell, ain't I made up my mind to my age? The ageless men is long gone; Pa allus said so. Flynn or no Flynn, my youth is gone. And now I'm in for it. Snakeweed. Well, it's worth it if he could be took away. He shore spoils the climate where he's at.

The sun continued its travel at right angles to Spud's course, swung low, and poured under his hatbrim directly on his face. A clump of green, so emphatic in contrast that it appeared black, showed beyond a gray butte. Rounding the butte, Spud came into sight of a flat at the edge of which eight cottonwoods grew. Around them, craving the sight of their leaves, a handful of adobe houses and shacks of gray, dust-scoured boards were huddled, with a periphery of haphazard corrals. This was Spareribs, a place where you stopped on your way to somewhere else. But here, at least, there was rest for man and beast, food cooked by someone else, and a corral to find your horse in in the morning. He rolled a cigarette as he drew nearer the settlement. He had the Four-Eye, too. That had to have a purpose, but he hadn't figured it out yet. There was a special place where it would come in; it might be for the purpose of alleviating Spareribs.

The sun had almost set when he stopped at the Rafter Lazy J corral. The boss came out, said, "Hello, Spud," and gave him the key to the hay room. Spud unsaddled, pulled out hay, filled the nose bag with oats and put it on the roan. Then he washed lavishly at the trough. The feeling of being coated with dust and dried-out sweat went away. He squatted on his heels, smoking, his spurs just touching his backside, waiting for the roan to finish his nose bag. The sun was down, the air ceased to burn and became caressing. He blew smoke four ways. This was a daily pause, a time of complete relaxation between the day itself and whatever the night might bring; he'd think about Snakeweed later.

When the animal had turned to its hay, he went slowly, lazily, down the dusty, half-formed street to the Gold Mine Saloon and Eating Parlor and turned into it. There was a long, pine bar with a moderate equipment of bottles and two large, imperfect mirrors behind it. Along the other half of the room half a dozen tables were ranged. At the far end a gambler dealt against himself at a faro layout. Spud took him in — dressed in the usual black, with a diamond in his tie and another on his left hand, but shabby and thin. You could size up the town from him. The barkeep looked like a barkeep; they almost always do.

Spud went to the bar and said, "Howdy."

"Howdy, stranger. What's your pleasure?"

"My pleasure's far from here." Spud jerked his head toward a bottle. "I'll take a shot o' red-eye, please."

"Help yourself." The barkeep passed him a bottle and glass.

"Can I get fed here?"

"We got steak and beans."

"I'll take steak. And another o' these."

"Help yourself."

The barkeep shouted through a little door, and pretty soon a Chinaman came out and laid the table. Spud ambled over and sat down. Four kinds of sauce in the bottles — long ago, this must have been a good restaurant. The Chinaman brought thin coffee, hot bread, a little bowl of canned peas, another of greengages. Minutes later he brought the steak. Spud ate steadily, industriously, without haste. Two X Circle X cowboys came in, then three Mexicans, drifting to the bar. By and by they went over to the faro layout. Spud could tell they were making about ten-cent bets.

There was a disturbance at the door, and Spud looked around. It was not exactly that there was any noise, only as the man entered, one was aware of it. Spud sighed. Here's Snakeweed, he thought, now things are going to commence. He finished his greengages and walked to the bar.

"Hello, Snakeweed."

"Spud Flynn! Why, hello, Spud."

"How about a little nosepaint?"

"Suits me."

"Barkeep, a couple o' fingers o' tanglefoot."

The barkeep set them out. They poured, raised glasses.

"How!"

"How!"

They drank. Snakeweed said, "Hell, that stuff's so much milk. Doctor, give us some Tiger Bone."

Tiger Bone is a Chinese drink, distilled from tigers. It is all but black, and it is dreadful. It is the backwards of Four-Eye Monongahela. I knew it, Spud thought, I knew it. I'm for it now.

The barkeep unearthed the long, strange bottle from a cupboard. He set the glasses out first and poured into them, not wanting a drop to fall on his hands and burn him. Snakeweed struck a match and lit his drink. Raising the flaming jigger, he said, "How."

Spud groaned internally. He lit his drink and answered. Snakeweed blew out as he drank, but Spud had almost forgotten, and he was worried about having his mustache burnt off, so he drew inward and gulped, thus getting the full benefit of it. He coughed, spat, and wiped his mouth with the back of his hand. Snakeweed just spat, without manners.

"That does it," the big man said.

Spud nodded. His pulse picked up, he felt the warmth, his perceptions became clearer. He saw that Snakeweed was a mite upset that he had been able to take the drink.

"I was hopin' to see you, Snakeweed," he said.

"Well, here I be. It's a pleasure to see you, Spud."

"I was fixin' to talk to you about a little matter."

"This is the best place in the world for it. Let her rip."

"Well, it's about a lady called Elvira Hartshorn."

"Elviry? Nice girl. She's a good cook, Spud. I'm fixin' to marry her."

"Seem-so she ain't fixin' to marry you."

"Maybe not right now, but she's a-goin' to, and pronto." Snakeweed paused and eyed Spud. "You know me. I'm Snakeweed; that's what they call me and they better like it."

Spud nodded again. That was Snakeweed's war-talk, that last statement. And he realized suddenly that he'd made his own, back there with Miss Hartshorn — Spud Flynn, come of a race o' kings. The Tiger Bone was burning in his vitals.

"I don't want for Miss Hartshorn to marry out of her own free choice," he said. "It don't seem right."

"Them's shore nice sentiments, Spud. But my marryin' ain't something I'm takin' anybody else's advice on."

"Maybe you're goin' to get it all the same." Spud's hands moved a fraction of an inch.

Snakeweed raised a hairy paw. "Don't think of it, Spud. Don't let it pass through your mind. You know I'd only have to plug you to keep up my self-respect. They ain't but one bullet will kill me, and I got it." He patted his cartridge belt, where the green point of the malachite bullet stuck downward among the lead ones. "Hashki Nez made it to kill me with, and I took it from him. I took him by his two hands and pulled him apart like a boiled fowl. That's me, Snakeweed."

Spud nodded. "Well, I guess that's that. Barkeep, two more o' the same."

Spud's willingness to come back on the liquor cramped

Snakeweed's complacency slightly, but he was still satisfied. Spud was thinking fast. He didn't kill me then — why not? Four-Eye won't fill him with human kindness, no more than Tiger Bone would make me mean. I might could get him drunk plain, and take the bullet.

Spud surveyed the man. He was hollow, they claimed he had a clockwork heart. You'd have to fill him up from the bottom. The top of his head and his eyes were small, but to get to them — each foot would take a full quart, a barrel for each leg, and two for his stomach — one for his proper insides and one for what hung out over his belt. Then you'd have to fill up his chest and his arms, and finally his face. No, it couldn't be done, not by any one man. He didn't drink to get tight, but because his insides itched and the liquor was scratchy. Spud looked at the face, the span-wide, almost lipless mouth and single, wiry hairs sticking out a couple of inches all over. Before they got onto him, the Navajos admired Snakeweed because his mouth was full of corn. His middle two teeth were black, the next each way red, then yellow and blue, like Indian corn. Miss Hartshorn was right; all the cowboys and miners in Arizona all drunk together would still be better.

Spud drank his drink and and sighed. "Well, I come a long ways. Guess I'll be turnin' in."

"Sorry to lose your company. It's a pleasure to drink with you."

"Tomorrow maybe. I'm kind o' tired."

"Growin' old, Spud?"

"I reckon. So long."

"So long."

Spud had half an idea to go over and lose some real money at faro; he'd dealt faro, he knew how that man felt, but he decided not to bother with it now. He stepped out into the soft, blue night, full of the smell seeping through from the bit of irrigated land beyond the cottonwoods. He felt at ease. He felt happier than he had since he sat on top of Polvadera Peak, two years ago, and decided that his youth had ended and from now on he was through with trouble. Not since then had his sinews moved as smoothly, his joints been as springy as they were now. At the corral, his horse rose with a surging effort and whickered for more hay. Spud threw some out to him.

He laid out his blanket and slicker, and reclining on them, his head against the saddle, looked at the stars and rolled a smoke. His hand fumbled toward his war-bags, touched the bottles. Not yet. He lit up and began thinking. I ain't but jest started, but it looks like I got to get me some help. Snakeweed ain't immortal, no more'n me. He's Snakeweed and I can like it, can I? There ain't room for the two of us in the Southwest, nor nowheres; if him and me fetch up in hell together, we're shore goin' to worry the devil. Now let's see . . .

He ran his mind back along his memory, like a man loping his horse along a back trail watching for something he let fall. Through years of days he traveled back, watching the sun and moon and darkness, the horizons and water holes and alkali flats of his time. He stopped at himself sitting in a narrow canyon with his gun in one hand and his rope in the other, at midday. His saddle and bridle were piled at one side. The horsehair rope lay on the ground before him, about ten feet of it from his hand to where it had been cut, and he was staring down the canyon at his horse, a fine big bay, running all out, and one foot and one hand of an Apache showing, the rest of the Indian hidden where he clung on the horse's further side. He was staring open-mouthed, helpless, with his gun in his hand. The cigarette he had given the Apache still lay burning on the ground where he had stood.

That feller was about seventeen ten years ago; he's the thief o' the world if he's alive now. He rolled the thought over in his mind, testing it, making sure that he knew this was it. Yep, I reckon I got to get holt o' Cochise. He looked at the stars. Late, that had taken half the night. He rolled up in his blanket and slept.

Well before dawn, he stuck the key and a dollar under the corral owner's door, saddled up and lit out. Four days, he figured, Indian business is always four days, I got to get goin'. He rode at a good trot, upward along a ridge, and so by sunrise had climbed to an outstanding foothill. Here he found enough brush to make, first, a good fire, then an evil-smelling smoke. The pillar went up, straight, high and thick. He threw on tobacco, four times, and two kinds of pollen from his medicine bag, and then in the column of smoke he placed a tuft of down from an eagle feather. The down rose, up and beyond sight; the high top of the column bent to an off-earth, favoring wind, straightened again. Toward the southwest, Spud noted, all right, but nasty traveling. He slapped the roan on the rump.

"Hop along, Sister Mary, hop along."

The first day was like the second, the second was like the third, the third like the fourth, and the fourth like first until noon. At that hour he came to a single piñon in a cleft of rock. The rock was so hot that it would burn a man's backside if he sat on it, and him wearing thin cotton overalls all but worn through, but the piñon made a ball of shade, a break, a change in starved, desert monotony. This tree bein' here is unreasonable, he figured, I guess I'll stop. All around was gray-white and yellow-white desert, with a thin, greenish wash over it of scattered cactus and yucca. One buzzard hung overhead. He unsaddled, and tethered the roan, otherwise the animal would have made a break for food and water. He lit a cigarette and blew smoke four ways.

"Here I be," he said.

The rock was a trifle higher than the surrounding country. Right smack in the middle of a God damn fryin' pan, sittin' on top of a hot button. This is a hell of a place to choose. I always heard Cochise was ornery.

He stiffened to attention, sending his thought out in the Apaches' own way. They were coming. Nothing could be seen, no change anywhere, but in a wide circle east and south of him motion existed, approached. He took the two bottles out of his war-bags. They were close, eyes and thoughts were upon him. He blew smoke four ways again. They stood up, a hundred men or more, lean, stringy, hollow-stomached, hard. Their hair hung straight, black and disorderly down their shoulders; on their naked backs, chests and thighs the dust had set in the sweat. Their quiet faces were full of ready war. One of them walked up to him. He had a single feather in his hair, and carried a rifle. The slender barrel with the bluing worn off and the hammer well used but in perfect condition, the scarred stock, the bit of turquoise tied to to the trigger guard, the readiness and steadiness with which he carried it, as though it had been born with him, the unindicated but inescapable relationship latent between its front sight and Spud contained the essence of the man, of all these warriors. Spud felt satisfied. In a mixture of bad Spanish and bad Apache he asked, "Where's Cochise?"

"Who knows?" The man stopped about five yards from him.

"I am looking for Cochise, and he knows it."

"I am chief here."

"No you ain't."

"Cochise is not going to talk to you, Amelicano."

Spud stirred slightly. "I am Spud Flynn, and I come of a race o' kings. I am here. Tell Cochise to come to me."

The watching Indians stirred, the headman stepped back. From behind their ranks a man made himself visible, approached. He stood seven feet high, a broad, strong man but not heavy; hard like the others. His big, sun-blackened face loomed like the head of a mountain, full of power. He had a shield and spear slung on his back, and carried an eagle feather fan in his right hand. He walked up to Spud and looked him over. For some time they watched each other, both thinking, both putting forth what they had. It was clear to them that they did not need an interpreter, each could speak his own way.

"I saw your smoke," Cochise said.

"I have something here," Spud answered.

"The Four-Eye," Cochise looked at the bottles. "Good. I take them."

"Maybe-so, maybe not."

"How?"

"I did not ride all this way to make you a present."

"One never does." Cochise sat down.

"There's something's got to be done. I'm thinkin' about something."

"My thought is ready to listen."

"Do you know Snakeweed?"

"Of course. There is too much of him."

"He needs to be removed."

"Remove him."

"Help me."

Cochise spat. "He is bad for us, but he is worse for white men, I think. Why should I remove him? I am fighting your people, I am holding my country for my Apaches. If he kills you, if you kill him, if you both die, we are pleased."

"He's plumb bad. He ain't just bad for you or me, or for everyone; he's badness. True Chiefs, no matter who they be, can't sit and let him go on."

"True Chiefs? Do you think you are one, white man? I have come, I have met you, I have heard you. I shall now take the liquor."

"I'm Spud Flynn, and I come of a race o' kings. The liquor is not yet yours."

Spud uncorked a bottle. The smell arose and spread outward, the Apaches swayed toward it, Cochise ran his tongue over his lips, Spud's mouth watered. He put the cork back.

Cochise said, "Njoni. We shall see."

Sitting cross-legged there in front of Spud, he pulled himself in, concentrating himself. His outer borders did not disappear, there remained the space which he occupied, but the essence of his huge frame, his sky-blocking shoulders, centered within his mind, between his eyes. He pulled in his power until it was more than pent lightning, and though he still looked at Spud, he was not noticing him. He was paying attention to that which he intended to do. The Apaches took cover.

The sun overhead stopped, waited, reluctantly crept back. Spud saw the shadow under which he sat swing westward, away from him. The sun was forced down its own trail into morning, it descended, hung above the eastern mesas. Time trembled. It was clear, he knew and Cochise was telling him, the fear over the hiding Indians proclaimed it, that if the sun went down backwards the past would come again, and no man could stand it. The earth was plunging like a horse being backed and fighting the bit, in a minute the earth would start bucking. Spud thought that Cochise had the thighs to ride it, but he knew he hadn't. His mouth was dry and he was sweating. In a minute he'd have to ask him to stop. Then he saw that Cochise was watching him. He got a grip on himself, and cleared his throat. Immediately, from old habit automatically, he looked for a target, aimed, spat, and knocked a lizard endwise. He nodded satisfaction, and returned his eyes to Cochise's again.

Slowly, carefully, the Chief set the sun back in its proper place. The shadow of the tree swung round, the earth quieted, the Indians sat up. Cochise filled himself again. His forehead was wet from the effort he had made.

"That is power," he said, reaching for the bottle.

"Wait!"

Spud spoke sharply. He had been scared, he was mad, and he aimed to be madder. He began swearing, soft and mild at first, as his custom was, then as his wrath stood up in him, he got into the swing of his language and the air before his face changed color. He used the deep cussing of seamen, the low, venomous cussing of cattlemen, the freighters' whiplike oaths, and what he heard from the Mississippi roustabouts when he was a kid at home. He cussed the cussing of Mexican muleteers when they're feeling fine and want to tell the world, and when, at the end of a long, desert day, a mule falls and spills its pack, and another mule steps on their feet. He used the dreadful, whining cussing with which Finn sailors can stop or start a storm, and his father's terrible Irish wrath, and Navajo and Apache and Ute words of shriveling strength, and coureur de bois talk, and Kit Carson's main oath on top of the lot, and all along through it he wove in and out the ideas that came to him, the voice of his anger pouring itself out full. The warriors ducked, raised their shields and touched their medicine bags. Cochise put his fan before his face, and twice he half raised his hand to ask Spud to stop. As the cowpuncher's voice died away at last, there was a thump on the ground between them, and the buzzard which had been sailing high above fell to earth, scorched clean of feathers.

Spud drew a breath. Cochise waved his eagle fan again. He was chagrined. He had performed his showiest magic first and overplayed his hand.

Spud said, "What you done is ornamental, but it don't serve no purpose. The sun always has to be put back. But this o' mine, now, it's relievin' to the feelin's. My throat's terrible dry. I reckon I'll take a drink."

Cochise made a negative gesture with his hand. He drew his knife slowly, and turning slightly to his left, reached up-ward. With the point against the blue of the upper sky he cut, the blade moving steadily through mild resistance, like cutting cheese. The four strokes made an irregular diamond. With his left hand he pulled that cut piece out of the sky, then he settled back and turned his gaze upon Spud.

Spud looked at the hole, and he couldn't stop looking. He had not known there was a blue like that, he didn't hardly believe any color could be so wonderful. The blue was transparent, letting through into more blueness, into endless depth. Behind the sky, through that hole, something was about to be seen. All happiness and contentment were waiting there. His soul went up toward it, he leaned forward, rapt, staring. There was nothing in the world that mattered if this could be attained. The desire of his innermost heart was about to make itself known. He would rise up and go to it, through the hole in the sky. The world was mean and small; this was everything. Sweet peace filled him. There was a date next Thursday — did it matter? Here was the end, after all. A promise made. But satisfaction, happiness, showed their full meaning to him. Who am I? he thought. It don't matter. I don't have to go on bein' Spud. His body had no weight, his whole being floated deliciously. A word of a kingly line whispered in his memory, a promise made. With an effort, he put his hand over his eyes. I'm Spud Flynn, and I come of a race o' kings. Snakeweed. He shook himself, opened his eyes and looked at Cochise.

"That was strong," he said. He still felt wistful.

Cochise put the piece back and sheathed his knife. He reached for the bottle.

"That was strong," Spud repeated, "but you didn't dast look at it yourself."

"What can you watch that I cannot?"

"Looky here."

He pulled a long piece of fine string out of his pocket.

"I was a sailor oncet," he said, and began knotting.

While his fingers worked, he whistled "Whiskey Johnny" through his teeth making a sound like wind in ropes, monotonous, repetitious, dolorous. The string moved, turned back upon itself, a fast plaiting with manifold knots. A web grew rapidly, strong, netlike, with a curious pattern in it. The whistling and the work continued. Cochise leaned closer, he was hardly breathing and his muscles bulged with effort. At length he put his hand out, covering the sennit.

"Untie it," he said in a choked voice.

Spud pulled one end, the whole thing came out straight with a little whizz. Cochise let out a sigh, moved his arms, swung himself from side to side, feeling his freedom again.

He looked straight at Spud and said in a low voice, "I was in there."

"Sure you was." Spud put the string away.

"Let us each have a little of that Four-Eye. There has been great work this afternoon."

"Suits me. Seems a shame to keep puttin' off a good thing."

Spud opened a bottle and passed it over. Cochise said "How!" and drank. Spud said "How!" and drank. The perfume of the Four-Eye Monongahela, its full flavor and its great strength pervaded them, filling them out, penetrating to their finger tips. They felt good-will toward mankind, they were elevated, their powers increased and their minds clarified.

"I never had a whole bottle of this before," Spud said. "How!"

Cochise took it in his turn. "I did once, long ago, but I shared it with Mangas Coloradas. How!"

They were superior to the world, but they desired it to be a better place, and they felt able to make it so. Spud's eye fell on the singed buzzard lying between them in its horrible nakedness.

"They ain't pretty even when they're alive," he said, "but this, like it is now — well, it don't remind me of a chicken dinner."

"Let us improve it," Cochise said.

He passed his fan over the bird, and blew upon it. It was

clothed again in its rusty black feathers. With an awful squawk it rose from the earth.

"You're plumb full o' magic," Spud said. "What I got's skill."

He pulled his two guns and fired each, twice. The bird came down again, stunned, two leaden bullets fused into shackles around its feet, two more in a collar around its neck.

"How's that?"

Cochise said, "Give the bird a drink, he deserves it."

Spud poured some of the liquor down its beak.

"What the hell's goin' on here?" the buzzard said. "You two can show off plenty power without misusin' me this way. Gimme some more o' that liquor and turn me loose."

"I reckon you've had plenty," Spud said.

"You do what I say, Spud Flynn. I know all about you. I know where you stole that roan you're goin' around on. And you, you big Apache you, I know where your life medicine's hidden, I do. You turn me loose and gimme another drink."

They said together, "You know too much." One reached for his gun, the other for his knife.

"Oh no you don't," the buzzard said. "I ain't the only one. What in hell do you think we do to pass the time up there, waitin' for our meals? You kill me, and I got plenty brothers to attend to you. The both of you."

"Free him," Cochise said.

Spud freed the bird and gave it another drink. "So long," it said, and flew upward unsteadily, emitting curious harsh sounds.

"It thinks it's a meadow lark," Spud said. "That's good liquor." He paused as an idea struck him. "Say, how did that bird get started talkin'. Did you do that?"

Cochise smiled faintly.

The sun was getting low. Cochise spoke to his men and fires were made, cooking started. An Indian brought a pile of small herbs, such as white men do not even see, for the roan, and a fire was built between the two men, but no one offended them with an offer of food. They smoked together ceremonially, contemplating the intimate, man-centered flame and the wide, universal sunset. Night followed close; when they sat enclosed within a sphere of low firelight, Spud passed the bottle. They smoked again.

Cochise said, "Now let us consider Snakeweed. My thought is upon him."

"For many reasons, any one o' which would be plenty, I've got to attend to him. I've made my war-boast and so has he."

"Good then. We have warriors here. Let us start."

"No, we can't do it that way. Snakeweed, he's got power, too. I jest want a little help to get around it."

Cigarettes were finished before Cochise replied. "I am holding my power here in the Apache country, I need it for my people. We win our battles, but we are few and hard pressed. One can win and win and lose in the end by going beyond one's strength. My power is here, for my people. I am afraid of letting my power leak out in a white man's affair, lest once it starts it all might run out. But you are right about Snakeweed, and Chiefs must help each other. What do you wish?"

Spud said gravely, "I don't reckon this'll wear out your medicine none. You know that malachite bullet he's got, the only one that will kill him?"

"Yes, Hashki Nez made it, but the Navajos talk too much. It was too bad."

"Well, I reckon there's a man o' yours can steal it for me. I'll tend to the rest."

"What man?"

"Feller who stole a big horse from me."

"We have stolen many horses, of all kinds and colors."

"Well, he was about seventeen years old, this Indian. I had the horse on a rope and my gun in my hand, and I was watchin' him, and it was midday. That was ten years ago. I figure if he's still alive he ought to be the thief o' the world by now."

Cochise smiled. "He is here. You are right." He spoke toward the surrounding fires.

A slender man of medium height came into the light. He was ordinary in every way, save for the fluid quietness of his movements. Cochise told him to sit down.

"This is he."

"And he's gone on stealing?"

"Look at the bottle."

Spud took it up. There was a drink less in it than there had been a moment ago. Its stimulation showed on the Thief's face.

"All right. He'll do."

They explained the matter. The man looked pleased.

"That will be good to do. It will be a credit to me. For a long time I have done just ordinary stealing; my people say to me, 'Thief, where is your skill?' It is good."

They gave him another drink, searched him, and took both bottles back. Cochise told him to return to his own fire.

It would take a book to tell what Cochise and Spud discussed as the stars moved westward and the bottle was emptied, as stars crossed over and they went into the second bottle. They talked far, wide, high and deep. Under the influence of the Four-Eye Monongahela they reached out and embraced mankind, understanding, pitying, loving. They touched on the past and the future, and poured wisdoms and vision back and forth into each other. It was a great night, a great talk.

Near dawn the Thief joined them to finish the second bottle. Cochise gave the horses four kinds of pollen, life, breath and a feather, and the Thief and Spud mounted. They could have run to Spareribs in a few hours, the way they were then, but being proud men it suited them to ride.

At first light Spud and the Chief touched hands.

"When you have time," Cochise said, "light your fire again and send a feather. Do it for no reason."

"I'll do that."

Spud and the Thief loped all that day and all the next night, at dawn reaching the ridge above Spareribs, and they took shelter in a mesquite grove. There they lay till the town awoke, and at last, after the sun was high and the air hot and dusty, Snakeweed came out of his shack. The Apache smiled.

"In his cartridge belt," Spud said.

"Do you want the whole belt?"

"Just the bullet."

"Good."

The Indian moved like smoke down the slope of the ridge. Near a stone he bent, pulled himself into himself, disappeared. Spud rolled over and went to sleep.

When he woke, well after noon, his first thought was, Golly, I hope I ain't slept it off. He sat up and considered himself. Reckon not. No. It ain't that kind o' drink. His joints moved supplely, his sinews were oiled, his thought danced as he considered life. Hell, I ain't old, he decided. What got into me? I ain't one that ages that-a-way. I'm back into it again. I'm Spud Flynn, I am, and by God I'm delighted.

He took it easy, smoking and thinking. Nice feller Cochise. Companionable when you got to know him. I'd kind o' like to look through that hole again, only I'd run a mile if he started to carve it out.

The Thief stood before him. "Here it is," he said.

Spud took the cartridge, staring at it. The malachite bullet's strong color glowed in the shade, it seemed to have life. One felt the magic that had been put into it.

"That's fine," he said. "Does he know he's lost it?"

"No." The Indian looked discontented. "I could have stolen him as well as not. And the place is full of good horses."

Spud nodded. "You'd like somethin' to take back with you, to show."

"Yes."

"Well, go ahead. The sky's the limit, jest so's you don't steal my roan or interfere with my play. I'll be through just after sundown, then go to it."

"*Njoni.*" The Thief hesitated. "How about a Mexican girl?"

"No. That ain't nice. Don't you do it."

"Good. I shall take just horses."

"All right. And thanks. All men will know soon that you stole the bullet."

The Indian smiled. "That is good. I shall go further up and wait. *Adiós.*"

"*Adiós.*"

The bullet was set in a percussion-cap cartridge. Spud went delicately about putting it into one of his new center-fires, fearful of losing the medicine, but when he had done, he saw that it was all right. The bullet was full of certainty. As the sun went down, he rode into Spareribs and put his horse up again at the Rafter Lazy J corral.

I shore feel fine, he thought as he drifted along the street. His spurs clinked on his heels, he was at ease, full of peaceful excitement and life. I am Spud Flynn, and it suits me fine. He would not eat now, though he had cause to be hungry; the Four-Eye still worked smoothly in his system, and Indian medicine calls for empty stomachs. He was full of good will and readiness.

To pass the time, he went into the saloon and strolled up to the faro bank. The dealer greeted him with the same weary, professional show of warmth he used on hundreds of such dingy, threadbare cowboys. Spud looked over the layout and the deck. What he didn't know about faro didn't exist. He lost a dollar, then put up two dollars coppered and lost them. The dealer had been handling dimes and quarters for so long he had to stretch his fingers to pick up the cartwheels.

"Try again," he said. "The luck always changes."

"Thanks," Spud said. "I reckon that's sufficient."

He walked out again, feeling pleased. It was dark outside now, in starlight the frame houses and adobes were less achingly bare. He made his way, leisurely, to the house with the broken front porch where Snakeweed lived. Looking through the window he could see the man gnawing at the roast hind leg of a bull beef. He stopped, picked a piece of gristle from between his teeth with a skinning knife, **and** went back to eating.

Spud felt just fine, he felt happy and that the world was right for him. Care was gone. Here was the beginning of pure pleasure. Standing a few yards away, he picked up a rock and hove it at the door. He heard Snakeweed move, and a chair fell over.

"What in hell?" called that harsh, roaring voice.

Spud loosened his gun in its holster.

"Come on out, Snakeweed you son of a bitch. Come on out and get it."